THE CODE

THE
CODE

BOOK ONE

BOBBY DePALO

Visit our website at
www.StillwaterPress.com
for more information.

First Stillwater River Publications Edition.

ISBN: 978-1-965733-92-9

1 2 3 4 5 6 7 8 9 10
Written by Bobby DePalo.
Cover and interior book design by Matthew St. Jean.
Cover photograph by stokkete / Adobe Stock.
Edited by Norma Sonstroem.
Published by Stillwater River Publications,
West Warwick, RI, USA.

Publisher's Cataloging-in-Publication
(Provided by Cassidy Cataloguing Services, Inc.)
Names: DePalo, Bobby, author.
Title: The code / Bobby DePalo.
Description: First Stillwater River Publications edition. |
West Warwick, RI, USA : Stillwater River Publications, [2025]
Identifiers: ISBN: 9781965733929
Subjects: LCSH: Organized crime–Rhode Island–Fiction. |
Italian American criminals–Rhode Island–Fiction. | Informers–Rhode
Island–Fiction. | Murder–Rhode Island–Fiction. | Betrayal–Fiction. |
LCGFT: Thrillers (Fiction) | Detective and mystery fiction.
Classification: LCC: PS3604.E6435 C64 2025 |
DDC: 813/.6–dc23

I dedicate this book to my family and friends.
And, especially to the ones who
kept our neighborhoods safe.

ONE

The tiny storage closet off the kitchen was the perfect hiding place, especially with the slots on the shuttered door for me to watch the unguarded family through. Something about standing motionless in the dark increased my heart rate and forced me to breathe deeper, which began to move the knitted facemask up and down my chin and nose, creating small itches that would normally drive someone crazy.

Getting in during the night was easy. Every loving family keeps a spare key hidden in close proximity to their favorite entry way, in case the children forgot theirs. When placing the key back under the plaster frog after entry, I couldn't help but notice the Hello Kitty logo on the keychain. It was cute. Innocent and cute.

Throughout the night my knees began to ache, and the tight grip I had on the hunting knife irritated my thumb and wrist; but from within my lair I kept still, very still, periodically flicking the razor-sharp blade's edge with my thumb. So much so, that it tore a small slice through the latex glove and into my skin. The pain didn't bother me; but the risk of any escaped DNA concerned me, so I stopped.

Loosen the grip on the knife handle, I told myself with my right brain, but my left side said to hold on even tighter. Motionless. Trance-like, ever so quiet. My eyes peered through the slots in the closet door like a hungry animal calculating its inevitable, yet patient pounce on its innocent and unsuspecting prey.

Little Nicholas appeared out of nowhere, entering the kitchen from the right and going straight for the Fruit Loops. That's when I noticed the oncoming sunlight peering through the windowpanes over the kitchen sink.

He had to stand on the chair to reach the kitchen cabinet, then retrieved the milk carton from the fridge with both hands because it was almost a quarter of his size. His footed Batman pajamas made the floor slippery, but he managed to pour the milk into the bowl without spilling a drop. I rooted for him as I squeezed the knife handle tighter.

"Nicholas," mom said, as she entered the kitchen with little Emma in hand. My heart rate increased faster as they passed extremely close to the closet door, me, still peering through the door's narrow slots. "Please save some milk for your sister."

"Okay, Mommy, but can I put my hand in the cereal box? There's a prize at the bottom of the box!"

"I want one! I want a pize too!" Emma yelled out, tugging on her mom's hand.

"It's pronounced prize, sweetie, not pize," mom answered, looking quite beautiful with the morning sun beaming on her fashionable and meticulous work clothes. A soft, white cotton top, a gray pencil-skirt, and dark blue heels graced her very fit, middle-aged figure. It was too familiar. *This is all so, déjà vu*, I thought.

"Nicholas can find the prize, Emma. One hand in the cereal is quite enough. Then you both can share it, okay sweetie?"

"Okay, Mommy, I guess so."

"That's my girl, Em. Now ask your brother to pour you some cereal, because mommy has to go to her back office and start her work day. I have clients coming in an hour, and I have to prepare some house listings on a few properties they may be interested in. So, please be good, the both of you. Daddy will be down in a minute to help you get ready for your day. And please remember what I always say, 'playing outside in the yard, gets the bodies hard, while Saturday morning cartoons, only helps out the loons!'" She walked out of my view, leaving little Emma behind. *Such a fine family,* I thought. *Such a sweet little girl, too.*

From behind my back, I brushed my hand against the dead bird hanging from my belt, then slowly shifted the hunting knife from my left hand to my right and quickly found the perfect grip. Being ambidextrous was a gift from God and I relished it.

I gazed upon the children while they enjoyed their Fruit Loops and retrieved their miniature puzzle prize, when the sound of footsteps followed by a boisterous voice entered the kitchen. My eyes stayed focused on the little girl as dad passed just feet from the closet door. I could smell his overbearing and overused cologne which was obnoxious to my sensibilities. Most strong smells were.

"Good morning, mia famiglia!"

"Good morning, Daddy!" they answered back, almost simultaneously.

"Where is Mrs. Carla Torro this fine morning, may I ask? Her handsome husband, Mr. Carmine Torro requests the presence of his beautiful bride! Where is she, I ask you?"

"She at work in her office, Daddy, and we are being good!" Emma beat Nicholas to the punch with her answer.

"Good girl, Emma. How about we go to the park this morning? You kids can bring your roller blades!"

"I want to go, Daddy!" Emma answered, jumping up and down! "I want to go!"

"Me too!" Nicholas said, wiping droplets of milk from his chin with his pajama sleeve.

"Alright, then finish up and get dressed, kids, hurry up!" Nicholas jumped off his tall seat and ran from the kitchen to his bedroom upstairs, while Emma worked hard to gulp down the last of the Fruit Loops at the bottom of her bowl. "Drink all the milk in your bowl Emma, then hurry up and get dressed. I'll start the car so the A/C cools it off, then I'll be back."

Their dad was gone from my limited sight while I stayed perfectly still. As the sweet angel crunched aloud and stared at the back of her cereal box, I calculated the distance between the closet door and the center of the kitchen, then slowly pulled the black face mask fully up and over the top of my nose, closing the gap in its eye opening even more.

Emma picked up the cereal bowl and drank the remaining sugary milk from the bottom. As she placed it back on the table, I pulled the top of my mask down a little more to cover my eyebrows, allowing two predatory senses to adjust and hone in on the girl's surroundings.

As the excited little girl wiped her milk mustache on the sleeve of her one-piece pajamas, I slowly reached for the doorknob. My hand found it in the dark on the first try as my eyes stayed seriously focused on the child's every move.

The curls of her dark brown hair bounced off her shoulders in matching rhythm as she hummed an unfamiliar song. Her smile was adorable. I gripped my big-bladed hunting knife tighter.

Slowly I turned the closet's doorknob, as little Emma spontaneously jumped from her tall seat and headed for her bedroom by way of the closet door of which I was standing just inches behind. I wondered how close to me she would come.

She broke into a small skip and got closer and closer, then she suddenly stopped on a dime and greeted her oncoming dad by hopping in his arms as he appeared just feet from the closet door.

"Hurry up little girl, the car is running and it's nice and cool!"

"Okay, Daddy! I will!" Emma then kissed her dad, dropped from his arms to the slippery floor and continued skipping away toward the stairs and on to her room.

Carmine stepped a foot closer to the closet door and peered at his smart phone as if he were reading something interesting. He turned away from the kitchen window's beaming sun, as he scrolled down with his right thumb, forcing his shirt sleeve to expose an enormous gold chain that looked like the links on a battleship's anchor. It was way too large for anyone to wear, even for the Italian "Cafones," (loud, no class) you see at the racetrack, carrying their life savings in their pocket, dying to show off a thick wad of cash which consisted of a hundred-dollar bill on the outside, wrapped around a pile of all ones on the inside.

And his pinky ring? That was worse. It was gaudy and tasteless. Something a carnival barker or a southern preacher with a mesmerized flock would wear.

Just as the putrid smell of his cologne reached my

nostrils again, I sprung from the closet like a big cat on a helpless gazelle.

With lightning speed, my left hand grabbed his left shoulder and spun him around so his back was to me, then I held him steady by planting my hand and arm across his chest, while I stood behind him with both feet planted firmly on the floor for traction.

Then, all in one quick motion, my right hand wielded the tightly-gripped blade around his front and across his exposed neck and throat, opening a two-inch-wide gash from ear to ear. His knees buckled and his body went limp, as I quietly brought him to the floor, laying him back and climbing up on his heaving chest.

There I sat. As the blood pumped and gushed from his throat, I lifted my face mask and looked into his bloodshot eyes.

"Do you know why you had this coming to you, Carmine?" I asked him again, as he stared back at me in disbelief. He tried to speak, but it was impossible to do so.

"Do you know why you had this coming?" Staring into my eyes, he attempted to mouth some words to me. It wasn't even a whisper, but I understood it all. Every word.

"Nicky," he mouthed, as the blood pumped from the gaping gash across his throat with every heartbeat. "Nicky...you are the godfather to my son, Nicholas. He's named after you. Why Nicky..., why?"

"You know why!" I yelled back, disgusted by the question as the blood continued to pump from his opened throat! "If not, maybe this will remind you!" With that, I reached around to my back belt loop and unhooked the dead canary I had hanging from a piece of twine.

"Do you see this, Carmine? Do you see it? This is why, you fuckin' rat!"

I held the bird in front of his eyes for a split second longer, then squeezed his two cheeks together to open his mouth.

"Open wide you fucking rat bastard!" His jaw was already dropped so the opening was wide enough. Head first, I slowly pushed the head of the canary into his mouth, as he looked on with water-filled eyes, then I jammed it in deeper so just the back end of the bird hung out with just two clawed feet and its pretty yellow tail feathers.

"Okay, Carmine? Now do you know why? Do you?" There was no reply. No response, nothing, because Carmine Torro, my best friend since childhood, the best man at my wedding and *my* son's godfather, was dead. Dead by my hands.

I kissed him on both cheeks and dragged his lifeless body into the closet, sitting him up so when they photographed his corpse, the canary would send a message for all to see. If you sing like a bird, you will die like a rat.

"Omerta," I whispered. "Remember the code? The code of silence?"

Before I left through the side door, from the kitchen counter I grabbed the cordless Mickey Mouse house phone I'd given the kids for Christmas and dialed 911.

"911," the dispatcher answered, in a monotone and rehearsed voice. "What is your emergency?"

"There has been a murder at 170 Dean Estates Drive. Please have your officers come in through the side door because the body is in the kitchen closet. Also, please hurry because the children are upstairs in their bedrooms and I don't want them to find their dad like this. Please don't scare the children, they're precious. Oh, and the mom has asthma, so please send a rescue too. Thank you, ma'am. Goodbye."

The next call I made was from a throwaway cell phone I pulled from my back pocket. I dialed it while driving out of Dean Estates and onto route 295. It only rang once.

"It's me," I said, as I looked in the rear-view mirror for signs of a tail. "It's done. The pizza is done. Well done."

Without another word I hung up the phone, threw it out the window and turned the car radio on. It was set to "B101-oldies." I leaned my head back on the headrest and took a deep breath while listening to Aerosmith's "Janie's got a gun," which was almost halfway finished which irked me a little.

Coincidence, I thought. *Carmine and I used to listen to this song when we were kids with small problems and big dreams.*

As I started to reminisce about our early days in the neighborhood, I paused, shook my head, leaned forward away from the headrest, changed the channel to a talk radio station and didn't look in the rear-view mirror again until I was almost home.

TWO

Pulling into my driveway was usually the highlight of my day, and I wasn't disappointed on this one either. I turned the radio off and skirted around the two bicycles laying in the driveway. My Heather and little Carmine raced across the yard to greet me, like two racehorses sprinting nose-to-nose in the last leg.

Little Carmine, I thought. I'd always hated that name, but big Carmine and I were more than friends. We were like brothers. So, when the two of us hid under the outside stairwell during seventh grade gym class, we made a solemn promise to one another.

While taking long, savoring drags on the one Marlboro butt we shared, I was surprised when totally out of the blue, Carmine suggested we each name our first son after the other one. I agreed, that was that, and I've hated my son's name ever since. So, I call him, Sonny.

"Daddy!" My Heather yelled out, above the neighbor's high revved and irritating mower, which never seemed to rest. "Carmine won't play with me, Daddy! He says dolls are for girls! Will you play with me?"

"Hi, Cupcake. Give Daddy a chance to take a shower, then I'll play dolls with you. Let me say hi to mommy and get cleaned up first, okay Cupcake?"

"Okay. See Carmine? Dolls are not just for girls!"

I ran right to the bedroom upstairs without looking for Grace and thought I heard her humming in the kitchen but couldn't be sure. Straining my ears to listen, I envisioned her making my favorite meal which I was tipped off to that morning. Chicken parmesan, light on the sauce, with cavatti macaroni and fresh baked, Italian garlic bread. The vision made my mouth water.

Then I envisioned *our* utility closet in our kitchen, forgotten, just feet away from Grace and in the corner by the refrigerator. It was dark, quiet, and seldom used.

After emptying my pockets, I dropped my clothes and rolled them into a ball, then threw them into the washer with double the amount of laundry detergent than usual. I jumped into the shower and scrubbed. Scrubbed until my skin was raw. But the thoughts of Carmine mouthing my name wouldn't wash away. No matter how much I scrubbed, they just wouldn't wash away.

I found myself stuck in deep thought under that hot water, spraying down hard on my tense and aching neck muscles. For how long, I don't know.

While getting dressed, my cell phone rang. The screen displayed the name "Uncle Edgar" but it was really code for Johnny Munaletto, better known as Johnny Moonlight, my Captain. I could never ignore a call from my Capo Regime, although I wanted to let it go to voice mail.

"Hello?" I answered, quietly and with my back to the bedroom door.

"Nicky," Johnny Moonlight said, rather than asked.

"Yes," I answered, in the same 'matter-of-fact-like' tone.

"I hear the pizza is done, is that true?"

"It's true. Well done."

"Good. And did you send that message we asked you to send?"

"I sent it."

"Good. I'll see you tonight, usual time."

"I'll be there."

Dinner was on the table when I got downstairs. Grace met me halfway across the floor with her usual kiss and hug, but the hairs on the back of my neck rose as I noticed the utility closet in the corner of the kitchen.

As I hugged Grace back, I kept one eye on the familiar shuttered door. I wanted so badly to go and open it, but I didn't want to give in to the fear. Besides, I knew that Carmine wasn't in there waiting to spring out and pounce on me or my family, but... *what if one of his crew is in there lurking behind those shutters*, I thought. *What if he's watching us right now? What if the order had come down to hit me tonight, too!*

I pictured Jimmy the Weasel, or better yet, No Neck Nunzio hiding in that closet, wearing a black ski mask that busted at the seams trying to cover his gigantic fat head with those bulging bug eyes, bugging out of the tiny opening in his tiny ski mask. *Could he even fit in that closet?*

"Nicky, are you okay?" Grace asked, as she put the biggest piece of garlic bread on my plate. I thought she looked nice but as usual, I noticed it, but forgot to tell her. I don't know why I do that. I don't mean to forget, and it bothers me when I do, but it just seems to happen all the time.

Even with her light-brown hair with dirty-blonde highlights, along with her big green eyes and cute little figure, I just couldn't always remember to tell her what a hot mom and wife she was. I'm working on it though.

I answered her without looking up, except for the one eye I had stretched up and over to watch the closet door that may or may not have hidden that big fat pile of shit inside it.

I never liked No Neck Nunzio. Mainly because he smelled bad. He was an effective enforcer and loyal Soldier, but always smelled like, 'Who did it and ran'!

"I'm okay, just tired from the commute home," I said, as I cut my veal into large pieces. "Living in the suburbs now is nice, but the drive home is tough. I'll get over it. How was your day, Grace?" Before she could answer, the phone rang a half of a ring before Sonny jumped up to claim it.

"I'll get it, he yelled, as he raced past the utility closet. With my eyes locked on, I imagined dead Carmine springing from it, with bloody hands feebly reaching for Sonny's little neck, with lifeless eyes and a whispering scream, emanating from the dead man's gaping neck wound. And, of course, stuffed in Carmine's blood-dripping and wide-opened mouth, was a fist full of bird feathers, just enough to choke a horse.

My thoughts were shaken by Sonny's reaction to someone on the phone.

"Mom, it's Auntie Carla, she's crying! Something about Uncle Carmine, I think. I can't understand her! Mom?"

After Grace took the phone and the shrill in my wife's voice subsided, I took the kids upstairs, got them washed and put their pajamas on them early. I stayed home the rest of the day and it flew by. And, as we listened to their mom cry herself to an early sleep that night, Sonny played with his monster trucks, while I played dolls with my little Cupcake. Then I went into the bathroom, threw up my veal, and laid down with Grace until nightime crept in and it was time to go.

THREE

I arrived at the strip club the same time Johnny Moonlight did. It was just before nine. His Caddy was hard to miss, especially the color. In his words, it was emerald jade, but in my opinion, it was baby-shit green. I couldn't tell him that though. Although I, too, was a "Made Guy" and carried clout within the family and beyond, Johnny Moonlight was a Captain and the head of our crew. That trumped me any day of the week, and no boss would ever take sides with anyone against one of his Captains. Unless he broke the rules of course. So, I remained respectful of him and his skanky-colored car at all times.

Johnny Moonlight was old school. No distribution of narcotics and following the rules was paramount. Although it was a shiny silver, he still had all his hair, making him look a lot younger than his age of sixty-four.

After the usual kiss, hug, and backslaps, we entered the club through the side door. Our eyes needed to adjust to the lack of light. So did our ears to the sudden shock of awe from the way-too-loud shitty music.

Strip club music wasn't for me. Never was, never will be. As for the girls? If you've seen one, you've seen them all. Hustlers, they're all hustlers, trying to hustle as much money as they can in the shortest amount of time before they get burnt out and leave. They treat every customer like a king, but as soon as the money dries up, they drop the king like a hot potato. It's actually funny to watch.

We made our way through the bar area, past the dance stage, and through the door to the back office. A small card game was in play but broke up as soon as we arrived.

Billy Feoli, the Underboss, greeted us with a huge smile—then me, with an even bigger bear hug.

Billy, who we called Billy Bath, and I don't know why, got the nickname when he was a kid. He won't tell anyone how. All I know is Billy Bath is the Underboss, second in command, and holds most of the cards. He's the hand of the boss and nobody messes with him. He's got his own guys around him all the time, too.

"You did good, kid! Really good! And when you called to tell me that the pizza was done, well done, I thought that was hilarious. I almost shit my pants; I laughed so hard! Isn't that right Johnny? This kid's a riot!"

I'm thirty-five. Why Billy Bath and Johnny Moonlight continue to call me kid is beyond me.

"You should be proud of yourself, Nicky. The job was well done. Just like the pizza! Ha, ha-ha!" He really cracked himself up, but I wasn't laughing along—just a smirk.

"Yeah, I am. Proud, I mean. Thanks, Billy." But it was a lie, I wasn't proud. I was ashamed. I killed my best friend. I stalked and killed my friend in his own home while his children were just steps away. I did what I had to do, but I was far from proud.

"Get Nicky a drink," Billy said, to no one in particular.

"No thanks, Billy. It's been a long day. I gotta get home to the family."

"Family, yes family. The family is everything. Don't ever forget that. Before you go Nicky, the boss wants to see you. Come this way. Johnny, you wait for us here."

I didn't want to go but could never refuse the boss, so I followed him into the way back while he continued mumbling to me about the importance of my family.

Billy Bath was the kind of guy that liked to preach old fashioned family values whenever he could. He looked like everybody's uncle, too. A stocky man, with noticeably large forearms. He fit the bill perfectly with his grandfatherly sweaters and bagged lunches he took to work every day.

But don't underestimate him. I once saw him put his finger in a man's eye and turn it inside out, with the inside of the guy's eyelid left protruding grotesquely on the outside of the eye socket. And all because the guy looked at Billy Bath's wife when they entered a restaurant on Federal Hill. Billy said to him, "Now try staring at her through *that* one from now on!"

The guy's friend managed to push and pop the eye back in but only after three guys held him down from squirming like a little girl. Billy then asked the rest of the patrons if anyone else wanted to look at his wife.

You see, Billy's wife, Petunia, I swear to God that was her real name, was thirty years younger than him and quite the looker. She dressed like an eighteen-year-old waitress from Hooters! It was a full-time job for Billy just to keep Petunia in the mink coats and expensive jewelry.

Most of Billy's ex-girlfriends were arm candy, while all of his ex-wives were trophy wives. I'll never get it. Billy is a jealous guy, and sometimes I think that jealous guys just ask for trouble.

We went through another door and into the "off limits office," 'the way back,' where No Neck Nunzio was standing by. He was bigger than ever and seemed like he would bust out of his clothes at any second like Bruce Banner transforming into The Incredible Hulk.

I told myself to exhale as I passed him, but I breathed in instead. I don't know why I do that and regretted it the moment I smelled that fat bastard! He smelled like the onions on the top of a New York System's hot wiener that was left out way too long.

The room was tiny and dim with oddball knick-knacks placed haphazardly everywhere. A picture of Ol' Blue Eyes, Frank Sinatra, hung prominently on the dark, outdated paneling. To the right of that hung a glass-framed shadow box containing three military service medals from the Korean War. To the left was a picture of the Virgin Mary. I wondered why the picture of Sinatra was in the middle, taking center stage and outranking the others?

I'd briefly met Frank when he visited the club in the eighties when I was just a 'Wanna-Be.' I was called to the back office and told to bring Mr. Sinatra a club soda. He thanked me, stuck two saw-notes in my shirt pocket and then told me to fetch his friend Jack Daniels, too.

As the lovely aroma of No Neck began to leave my nostrils, my eyes shifted away from Sinatra's portrait and settled on an old broken-down chair. It had hints of stuffing poking through the holes of the worn and broken down seat back.

And, in that throne, staring up at me through a haze of stagnant tobacco smoke, sat the old man, the boss of the family, Mr. Antonio Carlo Santini. The name Santini means "Little Saint" in Italian. I always thought that it fit him.

The powerful man stood 5'1" but the hunch made him look 5 feet even. His white shirt was wrinkled and faded a dingy yellow, and his overstretched suspenders held up the most outdated gray-cuffed pants I'd ever seen.

But the shoes? The shoes took the cake. He must have had them shined every other day, because the black and brown, nineteen-forties style wing tips were so highly polished, they looked like they belonged to a different person altogether when compared to the rest of the outfit.

His fedora was okay, but it was kind of squashed at the top and had either a blood or a macaroni gravy stain on it. The only thing that was worth more than three dollars was his Stogie cigar which was stuffed into the inside of his cheek. It burned continuously during his waking hours.

He was quite a sight. But the oath I took forced me to respect the man, no matter what his style. I also had to protect him with my life. I would kill for him and I would die for him. My best friend Carmine would have done the same, or so I thought.

"Antonio," said Billy Bath, as we both struggled to find room to stand. "Nicky wanted to go home to his family but decided to stay so he could talk to you first."

"Hello, Mr. Santini. It's good to see you, sir."

"Mannaggia, La Madonna! Come stai?" (god dam mother of God! How are you?) he asked.

Very quickly, I replied.

"Bene, bene" I'm good," I said.

"Please, Nicola, call me Antonio. No need for formalities, please, sit down. Billy, you sit too. Do you want an espresso?"

As he spoke with his hands, I caught a glimpse of calluses on his palms. His fingernails were dirty, but not from dirt. From soil. Antonio Santini was known for having the best garden that grew the sweetest tomatoes. Some say he also has the best fertilizer or compost buried under those tomato plants. Our Captain, Johnny Moonlight once said "Jimmy Hoffa is buried in that garden and that's why the tomatoes were so plump and juicy."

"No thank you, Mr. Santini. Espresso will keep me up all night." I felt uneasy sitting but did it anyway. I knew something was up.

"Nicola, Billy told me you did good taking care of that thing. And you left a message there too. That was good." Santini was speaking in code. Some conversations were supposed to be spoken only in code, but sometimes weren't, and some conversations were not to be spoken at all, but sometimes were. And some were mixed together. It's just the way it was.

"Billy Bath, get Nicola a glass of espresso! Come on!"

"No. Please, Mr. Santini, I can't. Thank you though."

"Okay, okay but next time."

"Yes, next time," I answered, nodding, and still looking up at Frankie.

"Nicola, I also know that you have been a good earner and loyal to the family under Johnny Moonlight. That's why we decided to promote you to Capo and give you your own crew. You'll be leaving Johnny's crew and taking over Carmine's old crew. Billy will work out the details with you. We have something we need you to take care of right away and I know you won't let us down. You talk to Billy and he'll set you up with that. Now come over here and let me congratulate you."

I was taken aback. *Carmine's crew?* Although it meant more money along with prestige, a huge pit formed in the middle of my stomach. *Not only did I steal my best friend's life, but now his crew?* I was already a "Made Man," a "Made Guy," so going from a Soldier to a Captain was no big deal to me, but I had to show gratitude so I took a step closer to the boss.

Santini set his Stogie down in his oversized glass ashtray from the 1964, New York World's Fair and reached up to kiss my cheek. Then he grabbed both my wrists and shook them hard as he spoke.

"You're a good boy, Nicola. We are all very proud of you for helping us to exterminate that rat problem we had. Remember though, for every one rat you see, there are fifty more."

"Thank you, Mr. Santini. Thank you for the opportunity. I won't let you down."

"You're welcome, Nicola. Now go home to your family." The boss picked up his cigar and tucked it away inside his cheek where it belonged. Billy, the good underboss, stood up too, fixed his trousers at the waist and walked me to and out the door, me wanting to gag while we passed fat ass again.

Unaware that Carmine's old crew, my new one, was summoned to the club right after I was, I stood surprised at the sight of the motley members already waiting for me by the bar. I knew them all. Johnny Moonlight must have known of my promotion in advance and asked them to show up, filling them in on it while I was inside with Santini and Billy Bath. It was an okay touch.

Micky Carella stepped forward and greeted me first. I knew he would. Micky was a charmer and had a way with the ladies. That's why we called him "Friday Night." Looking a little like a young Alec Baldwin with his jet-black hair and steel-blue eyes, Friday Night had more girlfriends than any other married guy I knew. If he had the chance, I think Friday would sleep with a one-legged, toothless prostitute as long as she had a heartbeat. I used to tease and tell him that he was hornier than a three-peckered, billy goat.

Friday Night got his nickname from something within the Italian culture. The maid of honor in an Italian wedding is called the Gumada (aka Cumadre, Cumada.) In the old days, because some of the bride grooms got caught sleeping with the Maid of Honor, any mistress that a married man kept behind the wife's back was labeled his "Gumada."

Because of this, Friday nights are known as "Gumada night" or girlfriend night. Whereas Saturday night is known as "wife night." To keep them both happy, you take the girlfriend out on Friday night and the wife on Saturday night.

Some wives with unfaithful husbands know more than they let on and become okay with the weekend arrangement rather than rock the boat. Just as long as the good husband doesn't get the nights mixed up and plan to meet the wrong woman at the right restaurant, instigating one hell of a cat fight. And, that, is why we call Micky Carella, "Friday night."

Bobby Castratoro, who we sometimes called "Bobby C" or the "Castrator," came forward to congratulate me next. He was a good-looking guy too but seemed to be a one-woman man. He reminded me of Tony Danza but with the body of a weight lifter. The guns on him must have been the same diameter as my thighs. And his chest? Ewe, Madawn! (Oh, Madonna—The Mother of Jesus.)

Next, came Mike Tissoni, who we called "Iron Mike." Iron Mike was bigger than a bus and nobody screwed with him. But, in reality, he was a big teddy bear. He wore his hair short on the sides and long in the back, almost shoulder length.

His face was a little rough and he could have passed for a WWE wrestler, but he was loyal and that's all I cared about. Bobby C and Iron Mike both hugged and kissed me and wished me luck.

So, we had Friday Night, Bobby C, and Iron Mike.

They were serious guys, experienced and as tough as they come. Lastly, to round off my crew, were two young guys with long, dirty blonde hair. The Saccoccia brothers.

The Saccoccia brothers, Brandon and Brendon, I shit you not, that was their names, were rookies, and each was as dumb as a stump! Most times.

They acted as rookies do and made too much of me by shaking my hand way too long and saying way too much. No nicknames for them yet. They weren't worthy. Nicknames aren't always badges of honor though. They can stick very easily. Do one stupid thing and it's yours for life. If those two dipshits don't get their acts together, I can just imagine the nicknames they'll end up with.

As for me, some guy once repeatedly insisted on nicknaming me "Nicky the Man, Mancusso," until I and a fellow crew member, Eddie I, put a stop to it by waiting for the guy to use a construction site outhouse. We then tipped it over on its closed door, trapping him inside his newly shit infested home, and left him there until I decided he had enough "crap" from us and let him out.

They just call me Nicky, now, except for the boss, who calls me Nicola. Eddie I was killed a few years back. I don't talk about it. Like Carmine, he was like a brother to me.

I forgot about Jimmy the Weasel, another member of my new crew. Jimmy has the nickname, Jimmy the Weasel, because..., well, he is a weasel. Plain and simple.

While everyone congratulated me, Jimmy stayed in the back, behind everyone else, pretending to be on his phone. That spoke volumes. I wasn't too surprised though. He had a bad attitude.

Jimmy could never become a "Made Member" because his mother wasn't Italian. Maybe that's why he was such a "Cucuzza," pronounced "Googootz," a "douche bag," who had a chip on his shoulder, always.

He never stood still, never looked you in the eye and never had your trust. His specialty was bookmaking with a little shylocking mixed in. As a rule, nobody likes a loan shark, but Jimmy took that to a higher level with his appearance and attitude.

Johnny Moonlight handed me a club soda with ice. "Congratulations kid," Johnny said with a half-smile. "Carmine was a good Capo but you'll be a better one. I hate to lose you from my crew but that's the way it goes."

"Thanks, Johnny. I'll miss your crew," I said, reaching for a napkin from the bar. I was really keeping an eye on Jimmy the Weasel, with his gray suit with white pin striping. A red carnation was usually sticking obnoxiously out of his shirt pocket.

"You were a fair Capo, Johnny, always had our backs. I'll miss that."

"Well, Nicky, now you have a crew of your own. Make as much shcarrole (escarole) as you can, who knows when it could come to an end. And take care of your guys. If you take care of them, they'll take care of you."

As Johnny spoke, I thought of Carmine, remembering him as he looked at me with those blood-shot and heartbroken eyes, mouthing those unforgettable words, *"Why Nicky, why?"*

Jimmy the Weasel couldn't pretend any longer and was forced to walk over to Johnny and me. As the only big shot in the gang who wore a suit, you could see him coming a mile away. There was no low-key life for him. He was a gangster and wanted everyone to know it. From his all-black ties over his all-black silk shirts, to his gold-plated um... everything, he just loved playing the part. I might change that, we'll see. It won't go easy though.

"Nicky Mancusso! You finally made it! The head of a crew and the boss of me no less, imagine that!" That was Jimmy the Weasel's way of saying, "Congratulations, Nicky!"

As a teenager, Jimmy was the type of guy that would steal money from the church box just before confessing to the priest that he shouted the words "holy crap!" when he didn't make enough money on his paper route to help his parents put food on the table that day.

After his confession the priest made Jimmy pray at the altar and say five "Hail Marys" and six "Our Fathers" for his sin, then the good Father would reach in his pocket and give Jimmy ten dollars of his own money to help his struggling family.

Jimmy would then run to the track with the sawbuck and the church's poor-box and put it all down on one horse, and if he won, he'd look up to the sky, thank God and scream, "holy Crap!"

Jimmy continued his bullshit by running his boney, ring-laden fingers through his fifties-style, greasy hair. "Hey, how did it feel snuffing out your best friend's life?" Jimmy asked, with eyes shifting away and a grin that exposed a gaudy, gold tooth.

"Did you make Carmine cry? That rat! I'm sure you made his kids cry for their Daddy!"

I took a huge step forward towards Jimmy when Johnny Moonlight intervened by taking the full glass of club soda from my hand and asking me if I wanted another.

Friday Night and Bobby C sprang into action right away but Iron Mike held them back. It was against the rules to put your hands on another made member. The Saccoccia brothers just stood there with their thumbs up their asses.

I wanted to put the Weasel's lights out right then and there but before I knew it Johnny had me by the arm and was walking me past the dance stage toward the side door. When I looked back, the Weasel was already gone.

Two girls, twins, named Star and Moon were dancing on stage with one hand each grasping the stripper's pole. One of them, I think it was Star, threw me a slight smile, stretched her neck out towards me with eyes opened wide and gave me a look that said, "Hey, I need to talk to you," but I just walked right past them both with my mind still focused on that douche bag.

I could never be totally sure how to tell those girls

apart. They were cute, kind of looked like china dolls. I was told that Star had a tattoo of a star and Moon had a tattoo of a moon, both on their right ankles, but I don't know, I never looked.

When I pushed open the exit door and suddenly landed in the side parking lot, it was like all of Fenway Park's night lights beaming down on me all at once. I had to take a moment for my eyes to adjust to it. If anyone ever wanted to "take me out" that was the time to do it.

"You okay, Kid?" Johnny asked, rubbing his eyes to see also.

"Yeah, I'm okay. I thought Jimmy the Weasle was supposed to respect my ass now. What's up with that?"

"Jimmy will always push it right to the edge, you know that. Let it go. How about us two Capos go and get ourselves something to eat downtown. Anna's is open till midnight."

"I can't, Johnny. I gotta get home to check on Grace. She's taking Carmine's death pretty hard. We've got her mother staying with us to help out."

"Okay, kid. Go home." Johnny kissed me on my right cheek, hugged me and patted my back, hard. As I walked to my pickup, I got my keys out and got ready for my usual trick. I was the only guy I hung out with who drove a pickup truck and still takes ribbings for it. But I didn't care. It works for me and here's why.

As I approached my jet-black Chevy Pickup, with all the chrome, bells and whistles, I remotely unlocked the driver's door and then purposely dropped my keys on the ground. This forced me to bend down to retrieve them but also allowed me to view the undercarriage of the 4-wheel drive with its impressive eighteen inches of ground clearance. Not that anyone would have a reason to strap a pipe bomb to my ride, it's just that it makes me feel better about having my kids sitting in the crew cab in the back sometimes.

All clear, I thought, swooped up my keys and jumped up and in.

I was still pissed off from that weasel inside the club, but told myself to focus on thoughts of Sonny and my Heather instead. I put the radio on and waited for the Cardi's commercial to end. Pleasant thoughts of Grace became mixed with unpleasant ones of Carmine.

Why did that idiot have to rat out the family? He had it made! He gave up Carla, Emma and Nicholas, everything!

What made him do it? He put me in that position too! He made me kill him!

I felt myself gripping the steering wheel hard, so I told myself to relax. Before I knew it, I was home, not remembering much of the drive there. I never did notice the song 'Sister Christian' that was playing before the very ending caught me by surprise. It was too bad, I liked that song, too.

The kids' bikes were still laying off to the side of the driveway as I pulled in. This time Sonny and my Heather didn't race to greet me, but that goddam next-door neighbor's grass clippings did. His lawn mower must have shot grass clippings over to our driveway leaving quite a mess strewn across the tar. *This guy was cutting his grass again? Is that all he does? What is it with these people in the suburbs?*

Grace's mom met me at the door with those, "I'm so sorry you lost your best friend, how can you go on without him, do you want something to eat, eyes." She spoke Italian and very little broken English. Maybe that's why she was so good at communicating with her eyes?

"You a hung, Nicky?"

"No, thank you, Aurelia, I already ate."

She just responded with her usual, *"ewe dee." (Oh Dio. Meaning, Oh God.)*

It was late. I went right upstairs to see Grace and the kids and it wasn't good. Grace was still crying and the kids were still up and in their rooms. Quiet. Listening. They sat still on their beds, terrified—as nervous as a dog shitting razor blades.

"I need to go with Carla tomorrow to make the funeral arrangements." Grace said, through watery, bloodshot, and mascara-smudged eyes.

"Okay, honey. Whatever you need."

"Nicky, how could this happen? With his babies in the house, too! What type of a sadistic monster would do such a thing? They said his throat was...," She broke down and flopped face first into her pile of disheveled pillows, sobbing like a love-struck teenager.

"I don't know, Grace. Maybe it was a junkie looking for something to steal to pawn, then maybe got scared off or something."

"It's just sick. Carla is a wreck and needs us now. You have to be a pall bearer; you know that, right?" Grace put her face back in the pillows and began weeping again.

"Of course, Carmine was my best friend! Grace

please, the kids are scared shitless. Please snap out of this. Carla and her kids need you to be strong."

As I walked past our bedroom window I did my usual eye sweep of the street below. "Did Carla say anything about whether or not the cops had any clues on who did this to Carmine?"

"No, she just said that the people who did this will pay. Nicky, why would she say people?"

"I don't know Grace. I'm going to get your mom to put the kids to bed... its late, get some sleep now."

FOUR

The next morning, I hurried to get ready and on the road, early. I needed to meet my new crew at Helen's Diner on the first day but may have to change that meeting site after that. Any connection the boys had to Carmine or his favorite breakfast joint had to be broken, quick. They were my crew now and control was big.

I shuffled into the kitchen for my morning caffeine boost when my heart almost fell out of my chest. Carmine and Carla's kids, Nicholas and Emma were sitting at my kitchen table eating cereal with my kids!

My eyes quickly shifted to my kitchen closet, then back to the kids. I looked fast at the cereal box, which was red like Fruit Loops but was quickly relieved to see it was only Sugar or Honey Smacks or something like that.

What the hell? I started to look visibly surprised but then caught myself. Sonny and my Heather jumped up and kissed me good morning, while Carmine's kids were a little slower, so I pushed them along by opening my arms wide and inviting them in.

They seemed quiet and I knew they missed their dad, so I pretended that everything was normal by tickling them a little like I always did. But neither one of them even cracked a smile.

Sonny, Little Carmine, spoke first to help me break the ice. He was mature for his young age. "Daddy, Nicholas and Emma are going to stay here today so Mommy and Auntie Carla can do an errand. Nona Aurelia is going to watch us today."

"Uncle Nicky, do you think my Daddy is in heaven?" Emma asked, hopping back up on her stool while reaching for my hand for help.

"I know he is, Sweetie. Heaven only takes in good people, and your Daddy was the best."

"Our dad once told me that he saved your life, is that true Uncle Nicky?" Nicholas asked, looking over at Sonny.

"It is." I replied.

"Will you tell us the story, Daddy?" asked my Heather, sitting up straight and ready to listen.

After thinking about it for a moment and without making eye contact, I poured Grace's famous coffee brew into the 'World's Greatest Dad' cup, and answered Heather in a drawn out and somber tone.

"Okay, I guess I can, but then I have to go to work." I borrowed the kid's cereal milk from them and poured a splash into my cup, then looked around for Grace's mom who could be anywhere at any time. I didn't want her hearing the story because she worried about everything. And I mean everything.

"Aurelia! Aurelia!" I waited. No response. She must have been washing or folding clothes downstairs or in my bedroom upstairs or dusting and then rearranging my bureau like I've told her a million times not to do. I loved her though, she was family.

"Aurelia!" She still didn't answer and I didn't like it. My mind quickly calculated the situation. Anytime anyone didn't respond to my call, I went into a defensive posture. Just something I did. Live by the sword, die by the sword, I guess.

Feeling uneasy, I turned with my back to the wall, glanced over at my kitchen utility closet and reluctantly began the story anyway.

"Well, one summer, when your Uncle Carmine and me...uh sorry, your dad to you two kids, and I were twelve years old, we would spend weekends at my Uncle Tony's farm in the country, with my four cousins, his three horses and a pony named Cocoa.

"Wait!" Emma interrupted. "Is this a scary story?"

"Not too scary, Sweetie."

"Okay, then," she replied, sitting up even straighter.

I continued. "Uncle Tony did his own farm maintenance because he was an elevator mechanic and a do-it-yourself kind of guy.

"On one hot summer day, we were all going swimming to a watering hole called Snapping Turtle Pond. Carmine and I couldn't wait to get our bathing suits on and meet at the pickup truck where we'd all hop in the back of the truck bed and cool off a little on the way.

"I noticed Cocoa the pony, standing at the electric fence wire and just couldn't resist walking over to pet her before joining the rest of the kids at the pickup truck.

"Well, Uncle tony had warned us not to touch the electric fence because he was experimenting in building his own charging system and when he first tested it, he found a dangerous flaw! The fence charging system was built with the wrong capacitors, meaning it allowed a constant flow of high voltage electricity, instead of just a safe pulse.

"Normally, if a horse touched the fence, a pulse could allow the animal to get off it in between the pulses, but a constant flow of electricity could paralyze it and stop the horse's heart in less than a minute.

"Plus, he found that the amperage was way too high!

"So, until he fixed it, he would only put it on at night and turn it off in the morning before the kids woke up. But this day he forgot to turn it off!

"It was a disaster waiting to happen because we were barefooted and the grass was wet from rain the night before. The perfect storm!

"When I reached over the fence wire to pet Cocoa's soft-skinned face with my left hand, I must have touched the wire with my right hand. The intense electricity, forced my hand muscles to contract and close my fingers around that wire in a super tight grip! I couldn't open it! I couldn't feel it!

"Unable to feel my entire arm, I ended up on the ground, on my back, looking up to the sky and watching my arm vibrate wildly like a cartoon character being electrocuted with its hair standing straight up!

"As my youngest cousin screamed in horror, the

other three took their beach towels off their shoulders and began whipping my arm in an attempt to hook it, pull it and break the tight grip that my hand had on the electric wire! But it was useless, their towels just slipped off my arm each time they tried. They couldn't touch me or even get close enough for fear of being electrocuted themselves!"

"Uncle, Nicky! I thought you said this story isn't scary!" Emma asked.

"I know, Sweetie, but this story has a happy ending. I promise, okay?"

"Okay."

"Now, where was I? Oh yeah. I knew my time was up! I knew I couldn't survive another few seconds, when all of a sudden and out of nowhere, my best buddy, Carmine Alfonso Torro, came running barefooted through the wet grass, and with both hands, grabbed ahold of my Monkees T-shirt and was determined not to let go!

"But, he must have touched me somewhere because he got a shock so intense that it sent him flying backwards toward the rest of the kids who tried to catch him before he hit hard on the ground!

"They missed though. But Carmine wouldn't give

up! Nope! He got up and came running at me again like a bat out of hell!"

"My Daddy's a hero!" Emma yelled.

"Yes, he is!" I answered.

"Emma! Stop interrupting!" Nicholas exclaimed. "Go on Uncle Nicky!"

"Well, by now, I was on my back, upside down with my legs over my head and my right hand still wrapped tightly around the fence wire! My whole body was vibrating, buzzing, and humming with no hope in sight!

"Carmine finally reached for me and grabbed my T-shirt again! Facing me and clutching my shirt with both hands, he ran backwards, dragging me and the fence-wire along the wet grass as he pulled. But the stretched out electric fence stretched to its limit and suddenly stopped! My closed hand still wouldn't open to let it go!

"Carmine kept pulling with all he had but it was no use! He pulled so hard that the metal fence posts on either side of me bent completely over, but still my hand would not let go of the vibrating and evil wire.

"All of a sudden, there was a loud, tearing, ripping sound as my shirt tore in half, separating me from Carmine and sending him backwards! With shirt pieces in his hand, he slid across the tar driveway on his bare back, leaving blood streaks on the tar and gouges of asphalt deep into his skin! He was hurt and I was still vibrating away on that electric fence wire! But did Carmine give up?"

"My Daddy would never give up!" Emma blurted out, then covered her mouth, not to interrupt the story again.

"It's okay, sweetie. You're right! He didn't give up! Carmine dropped his half of the torn T-shirt and ran at me again! He grabbed ahold of my half which was wrapped around my neck and under one arm pit. This time, he pulled backwards as if in a "tug of war"! The electric fence wire began to stretch beyond belief, dragging me with it across the wet grass again! I was dragged almost all the way to the driveway where Carmine's bloody track marks were!

"Then, all at once there was a loud "ping!" The electric wire snapped in half, breaking the circuit, and leaving the wire strand still buried deep inside my closed hand! The wire cut deep through my skin, oozing blood from just a sliver of an opening on my thumb side.

"Carmine and I were sent tumbling, each shirtless, end-over-end and finally resting side-by-side on the jagged and hot summer tar! Carmine was scraped up pretty good and I was left curled up in a ball because of my contracted muscles throughout my entire body.

"When the adults arrived, they picked us up and threw us into the back of the pickup truck for transportation to Snapping Turtle Pond where they soaked our bodies in the cool, shallow water. The adults tended to Carmine's wounds while my cousins gently pulled on each of my limbs until they eventually stopped recoiling like a curled-up garden hose.

"Uncle Tony figured that if I had remained on that electric fence for another minute, my heart would have stopped and that would be the end of that.

"So, the answer to your question, Nicholas ...is yes..., your father saved my life. And, yes, Emma, your Daddy is a hero!"

By now, tears were flowing down both of my cheeks. I took a deep breath and noticed Nicholas tearing up too. Emma smiled from ear to ear and my kids just awkwardly sat there, not knowing what to say or do.

I had to do it! I thought, turning away from the kids, pretending to be occupied with something. *I had to kill him! I had no choice! When the boss sends down an order, you have to comply! No questions, no nothing! Carmine would have done the exact same thing if he were in my shoes!*

I wiped my face with a paper towel and began to wash my coffee cup in the sink. *Besides,* I thought, *Carmine committed a mortal sin. He was a rat. He ratted out the family. He ratted out me! I could have gone to jail for life, never to see my wife and kids again. And, he'd be living the life of Reilly soaking up the sun on some beach somewhere in a witness protection program, somewhere in Shitberry RFD!*

"I had to do it, Carmine!" I said, aloud.

"What? What did you say, Daddy? My Heather asked.

"What?" I replied.

"You said you had to do something. Then you said Uncle Carmine's name."

"I don't know, Cupcake. Daddy needs to go right now." I ripped off another piece of paper towel and blew my nose before glancing at the kitchen closet again. I noticed I had been squinting due to a dull headache and throbbing neck pain. Then I realized that I'd been trying to block out that irritating and annoying sound of that running lawn mower from the neighbor next door, again!

"I have to go, kids. Be good for Nona, okay?"

Just then, Aurelia appeared and relieved my

worries and suspicions. I kissed them all and out the door I went.

While rubbing the back of my neck, I thought about meeting my new crew and some of the things I needed to go over with them at the diner. Reaching my pickup and without thinking, I dropped my keys before opening the door. Leaning over, I swooped up my keys and glanced underneath it. All was clear.

But something else was wrong, very wrong. My shiny new, jet black, 4x4 pickup with lots of chrome and all the bells and whistles, had wet and sticky grass clippings stuck to the side of the paint and chrome. And as I stood up, the blood from my head messed with that dull headache I was nursing, turning it into an unbearable pounding migraine.

I took a deep breath and saw my reflection in the truck window. Behind me, in that same reflection, I could see my neighbor wearing his wide brimmed sun hat and goofy Bermuda shorts, riding his fancy-shmancy riding lawn mower with all the latest and newfangled equipment on it. All except for a grass clippings catcher and maybe a nice, quiet muffler to reduce the most irritating sound a mower could make when you decide to run your mower seven days a week at all hours of the day!

I gingerly picked a single piece of grass from my lower fender and carried it across my boundary line, into my neighbor with the wide-brimmed sun-hat's yard.

I slowly walked over to the happy camper as he greeted me over the sound of his lawn buddy T1000 Super Jet, with a bountiful and way, way too happy, "hello neighbor!"

I greeted him back with a quiet, slow and steady, "shut the fuckin' motor off."

He looked perplexed, like the way my dog would look back at me when I asked her a question she didn't understand.

"Reach for the key and shut the fuckin' motor off," I repeated, "or, I'll reach for your neck, put my hand down your throat, out through your asshole and grab the key and shut it off myself, Neighborly-Neighbor!"

The engine quickly shut down and all was quiet. The silence was euphoric. I calmly and slowly continued. "Now listen to me. Do you see this blade of grass of yours?" I asked, holding it in front of his 'dumb-looking face.'

He nodded, "yes."

"If I ever see one blade of grass, like this one, ever again, anywhere near my truck, driveway, or entire property, and trust me, I'll know it's yours because your blade of grass will be the douchey one, I will bring it over to you, make you eat it, have you shit it out in your hand and then make you eat it again. Capiche? Neighbor?"

He continued nodding his head as I dropped his douchey blade of grass in his douchey hand and calmly and quietly walked away.

FIVE

The breakfast meeting with the crew went well. Bobby Castratoro, aka (Bobby C) and Iron Mike Tissoni ate their breakfast and blended in with the rest of the world. They were perfect gentlemen. But the two dumb-ass Saccoccia brothers wanted to send over their leftovers to the undercover Feds sitting two tables over, but I said, "No, not on my watch. We don't do stupid shit like that."

Of course, "Friday Night" tried to get the waitress's phone number and Jimmy the Weasel wanted Iron Mike to go out the bathroom window while a trucker ate at the lunch counter.

Jimmy was sure that the eighteen-wheeler was full of flat screen TV's just ripe for the picking. I said no to that too. I wanted to make a point. No stupid stuff, no drugs, and most of all, no drugs! I was from the old school and believed that we could make a decent living without dealing in narcotics.

"The old timers didn't do it," I said, "and we don't need to either. And, if I catch anyone in my crew going against my wishes, well, we won't go there." Heads nodded in unison. All except Jimmy the Weasel's of course.

"Is there a problem, Jimmy?" I waited for my answer as I passed the check down to the Saccoccia brothers. The old guys never pay and the Capo never ever pays. Part of the perks of being respected.

"Not at all, Skipper, no problem at all," Jimmy replied, with a slight smirk on his face that I guaranteed someday would be there for me to wipe off.

"Good, let's go to work then."

I needed to stop by the club to see Billy Bath, the Underboss. I was dying to know what job the boss had in mind for me.

The parking lot was sparse during the day because the prettier girls don't come on until 8 p.m. Even without a daytime cover charge, the club can't draw customers in when the girls are just so-so, or even worse, just plain old "butt-ugly."

Billy Bath's baby-shit green Caddy wasn't there yet, so I decided to wait inside. As usual, I went in through the side door and said hello to Sammy the bartender. The dancers call him "Scammy," because they say he tries to gyp the new girls at the end of the night when it's time for them to tip him out. He'd bullshit them by upping the fee and say it was the norm. I never liked him and since becoming a "made guy," I never paid for a drink again.

He poured me a club soda when he saw me coming and handed me a note with my drink.

"What's this?" He didn't answer and I found that strange.

It was taped closed with Scotch Tape, and I wondered if Scammy tried to read the contents inside. I peeled it open, tearing some of the note because of the tape. It was from Star, the china doll, the dancer who smiled and looked at me like she had more to say.

The note simply read, "Call me ASAP. I need to speak to you about Carmine. 555-0177, Star."

"Did you read this note, Sammy?"

"Of course not, Nicky, what do you think I am? Why would you accuse me of that?"

As I drank down my club soda, I placed the glass on the bar and slid it back to him with a fin underneath. I shouldn't have given it to him but I did anyway.

"Oh, I don't know, Sammy. Maybe because the Scotch Tape on this note has the same blue stripe on it as does the one on your Scotch Tape dispenser on your shelf right there. You know, like the blue stripe they put at the end of the tape to alert you that you're reaching the end? Do you have a blue stripe down your back too, Scammy? Are you reaching the end?"

"Awe come on, Nicky! Why do you gotta be like that! I didn't open... Oh, hi Billy! Nicky and I were just talking about old times. What'll you have?"

I never saw Billy Bath standing there, quietly, over my left shoulder. I didn't like that.

"Bring over a tomato juice while I sit over there and talk with Nicky for a while," Billy commanded. I put the note in my top pocket and sat with the Underboss in the darkened corner of the room. We never sat anywhere but in the corner, where it was dimly lit, and never did I ever sit anywhere but with my back to the wall, facing the door. Billy got right to it.

"Nicky, we need you to do something for us."

"What is it, Billy?"

"I'll get right to the point."

But, instead, he sat back and lit a cigarette before continuing. It was offensive to my sensitive nostrils and I'd wished he put it out.

"We need you to exterminate another rat. We've got a bigger rat problem than we thought, and we need to take care of it just like the other one. This time send a stronger message."

I leaned back in my chair to take it all in. Sending a stronger message only meant one thing. Instead of inserting a canary into the target's mouth, which meant the guy was killed because he sang like a bird, I would need to cut off his manhood and insert that into his mouth. It was the ultimate insult.

I couldn't show Billy that I had a problem doing anything I was asked to do, so I had to remain agreeable and somewhat eager. It wasn't that I had a problem taking out a rat, it's just that two rats in the family concerned me. The thought of doing life without parole wasn't something I was fond of either, especially because of a snitch. Or, a government-rewarded snitch at that.

Billy Bath puffed on his cigarette like it was his last. It reminded me of Carmine and me drawing on the same Marlboro while hiding out under the gym stairwell in the seventh grade.

"Who's the target? Not that it matters," I asked.

"For safety purposes his name won't be divulged until absolutely necessary.

"And you won't be alone on this one. This guy's a heavy hitter, so I'm bringing in Johnny Moonlight, you're old Captain. He will be responsible for the hit and you will assist him. Do you think you're up for it, Nicky?"

"I do. I won't let you down Billy, you know I won't."

"I know that, Nicky. That's why we chose you. You're a standup guy that follows the rules, especially Omerta," Billy said. *The code,* I thought. *The code of Silence.*

We could whisper the Italian word, "Omerta," but never speak of the English translation.

"The oath is broken more and more these days, Nicky," Billy said. "Some people don't honor it for life anymore and that's why we have this rat problem. Honoring the old ways and keeping with traditions is the only way to keep the family together. Follow the rules of La Cosa Nostra and it will live on. You will too."

"I know, Billy. I know."

"Did you know that in the old days, when the commission was formed and the rules were set, the word La Cosa Nostra wasn't even put to paper? The translation, "This thing of ours" was something they used to describe the creation by mouth only. It was to be kept secret and no name of the organization was given."

"I did know that, I replied. I'm old school, Billy. That's why I'm against getting into the narcotics trade. Its bad business and would rot us from the inside out. Lucky Luciano, the brainchild of the Commission was dead set against it and for good reason. So, tell me Billy, when do you want this done?"

"Tomorrow night," he answered.

"Ah mannaggia," I said, "So soon?"

"Yes, the sooner the better. We don't want the cancer to spread another inch and need to cut it out now. Nunzio will provide you and Johnny with two untraceable 9 millimeters, with the serial numbers scratched off.

You'll meet the target under the premise of a "sit down" to discuss the splitting of territories over loan sharking and gambling in the areas between his Boston and our Providence. Because he's a heavy hitter, naturally he would expect to meet with no one less than a high-ranking member, such as a Capo Regime. That's where you and Johnny Moonlight come in. He's a respected Captain and so are you now."

"You know I can work well with Johnny; he's like a father to me," I said.

"I know, but be careful. This guy you're meeting is top notch, and you'll see what I mean when the time comes. Let Johnny help you on this one. Then you call Nunzio and he'll tell you what to do with the body. You good?"

I paused for a second in thought. Then answered. "Okay, Billy. You can count on me." We hugged and kissed and I left the club through the front door this time. I figured I'd throw off the Feds in case they were set up to point their surveillance cameras on the side door as usual.

I spent the rest of the day at my construction company which was really a front for...well, everything. Grace was on my mind, and I wondered if she was able to help Carla make the funeral arrangements for Carmine. I thought I should show my face more at home before Carmine was buried, then I could focus solely on my crew, so I headed home a little early.

The Frosty Cone was on my way, so I picked up a half gallon of cherry vanilla ice cream and a box of Nutty Buddies for my kids, Carmine's kids too.

Neighborly-Neighbor was in his front yard as I pulled in, so I hopped out and offered him a Nutty Buddy. He started to decline until I told him why he needed to take one. He agreed.

SIX

As I got ready for my shower, I noticed the note from the girl named Star sticking out of my shirt pocket. By now the paper was wrinkled and more torn, but I could still make out the phone number, so I dialed.

I didn't know her very well, so it was a little awkward calling for the first time. Plus, I wasn't that kind of guy anymore. I wasn't like Friday Night, which by the way did end up getting that waitress's phone number at Helen's diner that morning.

He'd be all over an opportunity like this, I thought, as I dialed the phone.

In the old days, I spent a good part of my time fending off women, sometimes giving in to weak moments, and creating one problem after another for myself. Women used to tell me I looked like Andy

Garcia, and with that and the wise guy stigma, I could have gotten any women I wanted, but I learned my lesson when I almost lost Grace. I vowed I'd never be unfaithful again, if given another chance. It's hard sometimes but I'm determined to do it.

As I waited for Star to answer, I looked in the mirror and noticed a few more grays coming in on my temples. Grace says it makes me look distinguished, but I wondered if I should color them, knowing deep down that I never would.

Still waiting for Star to answer, I was reminded of the solid I once did for her when a customer stiffed her on a lap dance and threatened to slap her if she made another peep. When I got done with the guy, he was begging her to let him pay for ten lap dances instead of one, with a promise never to step foot in the club again.

"Hello," she answered, on the third or fourth ring. "Nicky, is this you?"

"It's me. Is this Star?"

"Yeah, listen Nicky, you've always been a standup guy and a straight shooter with me, and so I feel I should do the right thing by you. It's about Carmine, there's something I think you should know."

"What is it? What about Carmine?"

"I can't talk on the phone. Can you come by the club after I get off work tonight? I get off at 11:30 and after tipping out the bouncers, I usually get to my car a little after midnight. Can you meet me?"

"I guess so. Is this important, Honey? I mean, if Carmine owed you money...,"

"It's nothing like that, Nicky. I promise. Please meet me at my car, you won't be sorry. I drive a Black Beamer with a *'Just Live'* sticker on the trunk, and I park next to the dumpster in the back of the lot. Less scratches that way. You'll be there?"

"I'll be there."

"Thanks, Nicky."

After trying to scrub the remaining thoughts of Carmine off my body, I put on a nice set of clothes and sported my broken-in, python-skin boots.

It was a little hard putting my right boot on over my Walther PPK which was strapped to my ankle. The .380 caliber had a good-sized frame and sat in a larger holster than my 25 caliber Beretta ever did. But after the Danny Conte debacle, I vowed I'd never go underpowered like that ever again.

Why I thought I had to look good tonight, I don't know. I wouldn't cheat on Grace; those days are over. I got that stuff out of my system years ago, when I was young and stupid. But I still glanced at my wedding ring to remind me of what I had. And, I was good with it.

Grace was downstairs with her mother and the kids, talking about what everyone was going to wear at the wake tomorrow night. I could have listened but purposely tried not to. I wanted to forget everything about Carmine. Erase it all.

Then my cell phone rang with a blocked number displayed on the screen. I almost didn't pick it up, but the curiosity got the best of me. After the third ring,I answered with a low and uninterested, "Hello?"

The voice on the other end sounded a bit military.

"Is this Nicholas Mancusso?" I knew that sort of tone very well.

"It depends," I asked. "Are you selling Girl Scout cookies?"

"This is Detective Lieutenant, Howie Bergle, Providence police."

"Call me Nicky. Everyone does. What can I do for you, Detective?"

"I'd like to ask you a few questions about the death of Carmine Torro. I understand you two were best friends, so maybe you can help us clear up a couple of things."

"I'm sorry Lieutenant, but I don't talk to the police unless my lawyer is present. I learned that as a kid when they picked me up for questioning and then brought me home with two more broken ribs than I had before."

"I'm sorry to hear that, Mr. Mancusso...uh, Nicky. Maybe you'll call me if you need a favor?"

"I doubt it, but it was nice chatting with you Lieutenant Bergle."

I hung up the phone, ran downstairs and went over a few things with Grace before I left to meet with Star.

Backing out of the driveway I saw Neighborly-Neighbor raking fresh grass cuttings away from the edge of my property, in the dark.

It was only 8:45, so I swung by my shop to do some concrete work billing and maybe catch a quick nap before heading to the club to meet Star. I knew the next day would be a long one with the wake and the hit. I needed to be sharp.

As I rounded Dorrance Street, I noticed Friday Night's car parked outside Helen's diner. I wasn't surprised. I figured that waitress would have him coming around like a dog in heat until he got bored or the next hussy wagged *her* tail at him.

I decided to stop for a coffee but just for a minute. When I walked in, I saw the infatuated young waitress leaning forward on one side of the counter, looking mesmerized at whatever bullshit Friday Night was throwing at her, as Mr. Casanova leaned way back on his stool, savoring the moment before reeling in his catch.

"Hey, look who's here! It's Nicky Mancusso!" Friday gave me a long hug with a quiet whisper in my ear.

"Skipper," he said softly, "isn't she a knockout? Tell me she doesn't look like Farrah Faucet, huh? She's all over me like white on rice too! Do me a favor, Skip, I kind of told her that I'm part owner of a small movie studio. She wants to be an actress really bad, so would you back me up on that?"

I couldn't help but smirk, while I shook my head from side to side. It didn't matter because he didn't wait for an answer anyway.

"Sweetie, this is my boss."

"How do you do, I'm Nicky, Nicky Mancusso," I said, spinning the counter stool a little before sitting down. As kids, Carmine and I always liked to spin lunch counter stools before we sat on them.

I reached for her hand and she placed a tiny, soft, and delicate one in mine.

"I'm pleased to meet you, Nicky. I'm Dolores Belaruse. Would you like a cup of coffee or something?"

"Sure, coffee would be great, thanks. To go please." As she walked away, Friday Night and I both spun our stools to face each other's but also, kept our eyes on Doloris as she walked away. We just sat there in a trance, totally mesmerized, staring at the angel on earth.

"I call her, Dolores Belaruse with the nice caboose," said Friday. The apron strings draped evenly over each hip and tied at the back in the most feminine and dainty knot.

"Like I said, Skipper. Ain't she a knockout?"

"Friday," I replied, "She sure is that. But that stuff's not for me. That's trouble with a capital T!"

After scooping my coffee from Dolores's tiny hands and winking into her baby blue eyes, I laid a twenty on the counter, patted Friday on the back and headed for the door.

"See you later, Skipper!"

"Yyyyyup," and away I went.

.   .   .

On the way to my shop I couldn't help but wonder. Wonder about the job tomorrow night, wonder about meeting Star tonight, and wonder about Carmine right now and how he's doing in either Heaven or Hell.

Carmine's wake was tomorrow night at Mariani's Funeral Home which was across town, so I needed a plan to pay my respects, hang around long enough to please Grace and still make it in time for the bogus meeting and the ordered hit.

I pulled into my construction company's parking lot, unlocked three locks on the steel door, and clicked on the outdated fluorescent lights, causing a loud hum from the heavy ballasts above.

After making my way to my dimly-lit office in the rear, I settled in on the leather couch where if it had lips, it would surely sink my ships. But that was when I was young and full of piss and vinegar. Now I was approaching forty and right then just longing for a quick nap. I hoped that I clear my head of the things I've done and was about to do. Doing just that, I fell right to sleep.

SEVEN

Awake and yawning wide, I should have anticipated a wicked neckache when I hit the couch without a pillow under my head. I sat up. But as I rubbed the base of my skull and reached for my phone under some invoices on the coffee table, I heard something! Something that didn't belong! Then I heard it again! I wasn't alone!

Someone was in my shop. Slowly, I reached for my piece and immediately regretted wearing cowboy boots over my ankle holster again. I should have known better. I tried to squeeze just two fingers down, inside the boot and lift it out all in one steady motion. It was tough, but I did it without making a sound.

The lights were on in the shop and the office was dimly lit, so I had that and the home field advantage on my side. But whoever was out there certainly had the upper hand with the element of surprise. So, I quietly opened the door to the utility closet where the circuit box was located in an attempt to shut down all the lights and dominate the playing field.

Opening that darkened closet door gave me the willies, because I expected dead-Carmine to be waiting for me, standing there face to face, like a zombie with his throat slashed and his hands and long-nailed fingers outstretched to get me like a scene in a Freddy Krueger movie. But after quickly opening the door, I saw only a dust pan and broom standing inside.

Jesus Christ! Is this thing with Carmine going to haunt me for the rest of my life?

The circuit box was open so it was easy to find and click the main breaker switch off, darkening the entire shop including my office. The only lights I could see were the exit signs at both ends of the shop.

My pupils seemed to take forever to dilate and adjust to the darkness. I wanted to beat the intruder to seeing in the dark before his eyes adjusted before mine. Lowering my body frame as much I could, I held my gun straight out with my right hand and arm. Then I crept forward, slow, stealthy, silent. I became the predator.

As my eyes became accustomed to the darkness,

I felt invisible. Invisible to the world. And the power I felt was indescribable.

A loud "Pop!" broke the silence and shook my body to the core. Before I could think, my body reacted by involuntarily collapsing and making myself small. Then, I lifted my head in time to see the farthest exit door burst open, letting a vast array of street lights pour in and flood the room with light.

A dark figure, hunched over and masked, fled through the opening and slammed the door behind him, leaving me in total darkness again, soundless and still.

My heart was left pounding! I thought about that for a brief moment and wondered why so quickly? In days past, I'd have reacted to fear but never so quickly.

I backtracked to the fuse box to light up the shop for a complete sweep of the place. It was over.

The shop seemed clear so I called the Saccoccia brothers and ordered them to swing by. They lived the closest. I needed protection leaving the shop, plus I wanted a show of force in case anyone was still eyeing the place from the outside. They were there in twelve minutes with a sawed-off shotgun, two Smith 9 mills, and an AR-15. I was protected.

They must have called Iron Mike and Bobby C on

the way, because they arrived right after. It was a lot of force, but I was glad for the help.

Bobby checked out my truck's undercarriage for a pipe, while Mike made a final sweep of the shop. He didn't find any forced entry which worried me. It opened up a whole new ball game, because that meant someone either had a key or was a professional pick. Friday Night showed up late and, of course, Jimmy the Weasel was nowhere to be found.

Thanking the Saccoccia brothers was easy, I just peeled off a couple of C-notes and they were happy. The newbies were always game for big action and for little subway. The other guys wouldn't take a dime though. They knew the right thing to do.

It was a quarter to midnight, so I told the crew to stay by their phones, hopped in my truck, and headed to the club to meet Star.

The traffic was heavier than before, but that was normal. All the crazies come out after dark.

The club's neon light sign acted like a beacon as far away as Canal Street. The letters, "The Pink Pussycat" were in baby blue and the Angora cat logo was hot pink. You could see it a mile away.

As I pulled in, I noticed the place was packed. In the old days, only men frequented strip clubs but now thirty-five percent of the customers were woman. I didn't care who came in, as long they dropped a wad before they left.

Jimmy the Weasel's "look-at-me Lincoln" was parked alongside Billy Bath's baby-shit green Cadillac. I swung around to the back parking lot and drove past the back door and security camera. The lights became dimmer the farther I got from the rear entrance, but I spotted Star's black beamer next to the garbage dumpster anyway. It was parked nose-in and the *"Just Live"* bumper sticker confirmed it was hers.

Parking beside her, I could barely see through her tinted windows but my eyes quickly adjusted to the dark, and I realized she was in the driver's seat waiting for me. I was getting good at the "adjusting my eyes to the darkness thing" and felt a sense of power again as I waved to her while I hopped from my truck. My black truck next to the black beamer made things even darker.

Without thinking I flicked my wedding band with my thumb, after all, Star was young, beautiful, and resembled a china doll. And she wanted to meet me in her car, in the middle of the night at the back of a dark parking lot. Any guy would think he'd hit the 'Power

Ball.' Anyway, that was just my way of reminding myself that I was married so I flicked my ring again.

I hopped in the passenger side of her sexy BMW and tried to act unimpressed. Immediately, I averted my eyes as not to look at her stiletto heels and hot pink toenails below her long, smooth, and milky white legs. They were flawless! Not even a freckle!

The slit in her short skirt was flapped open and made them look even longer. Friday Night would have had a field day!

From her luscious legs, I raised my eyes to her bare bellied, midriff shirt and dangly, belly button ring as I awkwardly greeted her with a goofy, "Hey Star, what's cookin'?" *What a stupid thing to say,* I quickly told myself.

I felt like an idiot, taking my eyes off her body and onto her silky-smooth face where they belonged. I tried again.

"How have you been, Star." This time I looked her right in the eyes. The only problem was, one of them had a six-inch knife handle sticking straight out of it! The blade was completely imbedded in her left eye as she faced me with her wide opened and baby blue right!

I jumped back 6 inches or so before hitting the

inside of her tiny beamer and squirmed a little before settling down and lifting my pant leg that covered my hand gun, getting ready for who knows what!

Motionless, with nowhere to retreat, I just sat there, Star staring back at me with the most peculiar look on her face. Yet, there was no blood. No blood to ruin that perfect doll face! It must have drained to the back of her skull because of the way her head was tilted back.

Oh, Madonna mia! Star, what did you get yourself into? Who did this to you? If you owed Carmine money, well, he sure didn't come back from the dead and drive a knife blade into your skull to collect it!

After what seemed like minutes, I looked around before opening the car door. Then, I wiped down both the inside and outside door handles with my shirt sleeve and everywhere else I may have touched.

One last look at Star was my way of paying respect to her before getting in my truck and driving away. I glanced in my rear-view mirror most of the way home, feeling like I was doing that a lot more lately.

EIGHT

Grace was asleep when I got home. I removed my clothes, dropped them on the floor, and then rolled them up in a ball before throwing them into the washer. With extra detergent, as usual.

The shower was always my best place to think, so I lathered myself up, leaned against the tiles and let the hot water rain down on me, as I replayed the week's events. Starting with Carmine, my best friend.

I remembered getting the call from Johnny Moonlight last week and reflected on that. As the water ran down my face and eyelids, I recalled when my then Captain told me to meet him in front of the duck pond at Roger Williams Park Zoo. Johnny used to like to sit and feed the ducks there, so I grabbed the half-eaten bag of Italian bread from the bread box on my kitchen counter before I left. I didn't want to go empty handed.

After arriving, Johnny and I exchanged kisses, hugs, backslaps, and pleasantries before getting right to it. As I recalled, the meeting went something like this.

"Nicky, you've been like a son to me all these years, you know that, right?" I reached into my bread bag and threw a small piece into the water where forty-thousand birds, ducks, chickens, and I don't know what the Christ else, all swam and fought to kill each other for one tiny morsel of bread.

You enjoy doing this? I thought, watching one little chick get picked on by three bigger ones, as it tried to swim in front of the rest of the group.

"And you've been like a father to me too, Johnny." I answered. "Why, what's up? What do you need from me?"

"I've got some bad news, Kid, and I don't know how to tell you. It's going to crush you, Nicky. It's about Carmine."

"Johnny, listen, you always used to say that there was nothing in this world that Nicky Mancusso and Carmine Torro couldn't conquer together, so this should be just another piece of cake, right?"

"Not this time," Johnny said, throwing another

piece of bread into what looked like a piranha frenzy that took place the moment the bread left his hand.

I sat back against the park bench and closed the bag. "Just say it, Johnny. Just tell me."

"Alright, I will. Our police informant tells us that your best friend, Carmine Torro, has been working with the Feds for at least a month. Feeding them the details on our loan sharking and gambling operations for all of New England. The Feds also have him on tape agreeing to wear a wire. Carmine's also heard on it telling the agent about the sports betting operation he headed last winter."

I didn't say a word. I just stared back at my Capo, Johnny Moonlight. He continued to speak.

"He's also provided the Feds with a hundred-man list of who's who. You're on that list, Nicky. We don't know if they offered him money for his testimony or he may have been pinched from a bust that we don't know about. We are not sure who approached who.

"Our informant also told us that Carmine has made a deal to be put into the Witness Protection Program and has requested relocating to a warm and sunny climate where he can sit by the pool in a gated community for retired people. Carla and the two kids are all for it and are going with him. They've requested some small nowhere town in Ari-fuckin-zona, in exchange for his testimony against the family. Your best friend is a rat, Nicky. A fuckin' rat!"

I didn't react. I just sat, stoic, staring at the flock of ducks and imagining myself pulling out my piece and opening fire into the entire flock. I pictured all the elegant, pure white and pretty birds now spattered in dark red blood, with thousands of detached feathers floating endlessly in the air, as I methodically reloaded and killed some more.

But instead of acting out my fantasy, I reached into my bread bag and broke three slices into many small pieces and threw them all into the lake away from the group, allowing the weaker and smaller birds a chance to find a morsel without just the stronger ones prevailing.

"Are you okay, kid?"

"I'm okay."

"I know it's hard to swallow. That's why I took you here. This place always brings me some peace and solitude. I'm sorry it was Carmine, Nicky. I know what he means to you."

I sat by the edge of that lake, motionless, with no emotions, just gazing into that flock of ducks while they swam back and forth, waiting for our next move.

"There's more," Johnny said, without looking up. I waited. "The rat problem has to be taken care of and the boss wants you to do it, Nicky. You're the only guy that can get close to him. Capiche?"

I thought about it without looking up, then I responded.

"I understand, Johnny. Capiche," I replied.

I could never refuse anyway or else *I* would be killed.

The shower-water continued to rain down on my head as I continued to remember. I must have been under the water longer than I thought because the temperature started to get cold. I turned the arrow on the knob further to "hot" and it was better but forced me to replay more. More of the same.

I started to recall stuffing the canary into Carmine's mouth but was able to wash it all away with a head shake and a direct blast of water on my tired face.

If I let myself, I would grieve over my friend's death. Instead, I rinsed off, hopped out, dried myself and brushed my teeth. More time to think.

What did Star need to tell me and why was she whacked the same night she was to meet with me? Was it a coincidence? I doubt it.

Exhausted, I jumped into bed, held onto my wife, and fell quickly to sleep. I needed it.

. . .

The next morning came fast. It was 10 a.m. I needed to call in to Billy Bath to get the word on Star's murder at the club and anything else I could learn about what she knew about Carmine, without letting on that I ever met with her.

Grace was ironing clothes for the kids to wear to their first funeral. We felt that the funeral mass was okay but they were still too young for a wake, especially if they made Carmine look presentable enough for an open casket. We didn't think they were ready for a showing yet.

Little Carmine knocked at my bedroom door as I was getting ready.

"Dad!"

"Yes, Sonny?"

"There's a lieutenant somebody at the front door!"

"Don't let him in yet, Sonny! I'll be right down!"

Well, that definitely didn't take long, I thought, as I hurried to finish dressing. I made a mental note of my clothes in the wash and made sure I didn't forget and leave any of Star's DNA on anything. I didn't want to get pinched for a hit that I didn't do.

I ran downstairs and found Grace offering the lieutenant a cup of coffee at the kitchen table. I've told her a thousand times never to let a cop in without a search warrant but, forget it.

The detective showed me his I.D. and badge. Howard Bergle, number 642 and immediately started peppering me with questions about a girl named Star that worked in the club that I frequented.

But before he got too far, I put my hand up, showed him the palm of my hand and asked to see a warrant. He said it was just a social visit, so with that I showed him the door. Grace could tell I wasn't happy.

The cop stood and agreed to leave without a fight, thanking Grace for the coffee he almost had. "Oh, just one last thing before I go," said Bergle, as he stopped, turned, and stood in the doorway.

"Is there any reason why this girl Star, who incidentally was found murdered last night, made a phone call to you on the night in question? Phone records don't lie, Mr. Mancusso." My wife immediately turned to me and looked into my eyes, deeply— searching for answers upon my poker-faced face.

His fake question showed me the guy's true

character. Any man that would risk hurting a man's wife just to throw in a dig isn't a real man. In my book he's a 'pezza di merda' (piece of shit).

Without even blinking, I showed him the palm of my hand again and said, "Too bad you couldn't stay, my wife makes one hell of a cup of coffee."

As I closed the door on the nice detective, I could see Neighborly-Neighbor in the far background stretching his nosy neck out to get a better look from the seat of his riding mower as he drove past Bergle. The mower's irritating buzz was already going through my head and starting to give me a slight headache. I closed the door tightly and secured both locks.

I finished getting ready, then downed Grace's coffee and homemade, sugar-sprinkled doughboy. She made the best doughboys.

I needed to meet up with Johnny Moonlight to discuss the hit tonight and also to get the "nines" from No Neck Nunzio.

The nine-millimeter was our weapon of choice. Light, fairly small and enough energy to stop a small bull at fifty yards. Then I had to meet Grace at the funeral parlor and spend at least an hour grieving over my best friend's untimely death. And from there it was on to that other rat problem and hopefully, just hopefully, get back in time to cuddle with my wife and enjoy a much-needed and good-night's sleep.

After kissing Grace goodbye, I headed for my vehicle and dropped my keys. Then, after the key swoop and quick inspection, I slowly stood back up to the sound of that constant and annoying lawn mower!

There wasn't even one douchey grass blade stuck to my truck this time, but still, that annoying sound prevented me from hopping in and just driving away. I just couldn't let it go.

So, I took a deep breath, stepped over his cutesy little daffodils that separated his yard from mine and headed for Neighborly-Neighbor in a deliberate and straight line. He wore his usual wide-brimmed sun hat with his goofy Bermuda shorts, only this time he sported a brand-new pair of lime-green clogs. His outfit clashed so much that he looked like he purposely wore it just to aggravate..., the world.

When Neighborly-Neighbor saw me coming, he stopped the mower abruptly, and started to shout out his huge and annoying, "hello neighbor!" before stopping himself midstream and shutting off his T1000 Super Jet, immediately! He knew the routine.

"Um, good morning," I said.

He just nodded.

"Did you enjoy the Nutty Buddy that I left you yesterday?"

He nodded a little faster this time.

"Good. Now, here's the deal. I'm trying to be a good neighbor, I really am. And, I'm trying to like you. It's just that..., well. It's like this.

From now on, you will *not* run your lawn mower on T's and S's. That means, any day of the week that starts with either the letter T or the letter S, is off limits to cutting your grass that day. I'm trying to help you here, okay?"

He nodded even faster. "Now, I don't have to tell you what will happen to you if I find out you violated the T's and S's Ordinance, do I?"

With eyes wide open and mouth closed shut, he shook his head, "no."

"Okay then, in that case, I'll let you continue to give me a big, neighborly "Hello!" when you see me. Would you like that?"

He nodded a slow but confused "yes."

"Good, now have yourself a great day, neighbor! Oh, by the way, today's Tuesday." He stared back, nodding. "So, get the fuck off that fuckin' thing before I snap your fuckin' neck!"

NINE

My plan was to meet with each member of my crew to set things straight going forward. I met with Friday Night at Helen's diner first. I figured he'd be there, well, until that waitress got tired of his bullshit anyway, or his wife barged in, unannounced, with a frying pan in one hand and a kitchen knife in the other.

Friday and I talked about things I wanted done going forward with the gambling operation. I also wanted him to get a couple more guys on board to increase our revenue, especially with football season coming up.

It was a short but productive meeting and I must say that Friday Night did focus on my needs rather than the Caboose on Dolores Belaruse. Either he was getting tired of her or she was starting to catch on to his movie producing baloney? I didn't stay long.

I stopped on the way to the club and got a haircut. Sitting in the barber's chair always gave me some time to think, which I appreciated.

Star was foremost on my mind. And then, of course, Carmine. I sometimes let the barber give me a hot towel and a shave, plus, my barber also helps collect bets for me, so it was business mixed with pleasure. I enjoyed the hot towel.

I made it to The Pink Pussycat or the "Cat," as we called it, just in time. Johnny Moonlight was already there talking to Billy Bath, Iron Mike, Bobby Castratoro and, of course, No Neck who was there to provide Johnny and me with the nines in private.

Besides No Neck, the rest of the crew would have no knowledge of the hit that we were preparing for tonight unless the boss wanted it that way.

As I approached, I'm sure they were talking about Star's murder and the break-in at my construction office last night.

After I greeted everyone, we all made our way through the usual barrage of customers and past the dance stage. That's when I saw Scammy standing behind the bar through the corner of my eye. When I looked his way, he wouldn't look at me, and I picked up on that right away.

Before entering the back room, I glanced back at the stage, imagining seeing Star and her sister Moon hanging on to that stripper pole, looking like two cute china dolls, but instead there was just Devon, dancing to some song I didn't know or like and couldn't understand the words to.

"Does anyone have any knowledge as to who whacked this girl last night?" Billy said, with some authority in his voice. We all looked at each other first before shaking our heads at the same time.

"Well, we can't have that shit here, it's bad for business. We need to stay under the radar. No Feds, no cops, no nothing!"

"It was probably some bat-shit crazy customer that didn't quite like the way the girl turned him down when he fell in love with her after his first three-minute lap dance. Happens all the time. The girl is nice to them and these guys want to take them home and marry them for life. Little did they know the chick is just in it for the money.

The cops will probably hang around here for a few more days but if everyone keeps it cool, we have nothing to worry about."

Billy suddenly turned to me. "Nicky, what about you?" I panicked for a second. *Does he know that I was here to meet Star about Carmine last night?* I was caught off guard and couldn't think of what to say! I wasn't about to tell everyone that I sat next to her in her Beamer while she had a six-inch knife sticking out of her eye socket. I still needed to find out what she knew about Carmine and why it was so important to tell me. And, of course, why she was whacked in the process. But Billy pointing to me was very unnerving.

"Uh, what do you mean, Billy? I don't...,"

He interrupted. "I hear you had some trouble last night? "A break-in or something at your shop?"

Phew! I just dodged a bullet and was sure he was asking me about the murder! I regained my composure and then answered the way I should have. Calm and cool like always.

"It was nothing. Someone tried to break in, but I scared them off before they got anything."

"Okay," said Billy. "Maybe it was a junky looking for some scrap to pawn. Alright, I have some business with Johnny and Nicky, so all of you except Nunzio need to leave us. We'll talk later."

We followed the underboss into the back office where Santini resided but he wasn't in. Billy sat at the boss's desk which I thought was unusual but what do I know.

"Alright, Nunzio. Hand them the pieces, show what you have to show and then leave us." I knew then that No Neck had no idea who the target was either. He pulled out two, Rossi nine-millimeter semi-autos from a burlap sack. As he got closer to us, I could smell that fat bastard.

"These guns are 'Throw-aways,'" No Neck said, as he raised one of them in the air. "I taped the pistol grip and the trigger with my magic tape so no finger-prints will be left on it. The serial numbers have been filed off so just chuck them out the window on the way home." Then, without another word, No Neck left us, but his odor remained.

Johnny Moonlight asked Billy Bath the burning question before I did. I was dying to know.

"Who's the target, Billy? I know he's a heavy hitter but for the life of me I can't guess who the rat is this time."

Billy sat back in Santini's stitch-split chair and answered Johnny slowly.

"For security reasons and also the element of surprise, you won't know who the target is until you arrive at the destination. The meeting between him and the two of you is tonight at seven, sharp!"

"Oh, and we want to send a stronger message on this one. No canary this time. Leave a rat. We want you to stuff a rat so far down the throat of that piece of shit that just the tail sticks out! Pick it up from Nunzio on the way out. Capiche?"

"Capiche," we both answered.

No man parts? I thought. I didn't know which was worse, pushing a rat down the guy's throat or cutting off his pecker and messing with that! I decided to do whatever I was told and don't think about it.

After getting the address and the rest of the details, we met No Neck at the back door. He handed us another sack with a large lump in it. We peaked, of course. I have to say, it contained the biggest rat I had ever seen! It was dead though, thank God!

No Neck finally spoke. "I got it frozen now but it should be thawed out by the time you need it."

I whispered to Johnny as he took the rat sack from No Neck. "How the Hell are we going to get that big thing in that guy's mouth?"

Johnny shook his head but showed no emotion, so I put the nine-millimeter in a back-belt holster under my shirt and I think Johnny did the same.

I still had to meet Grace at the wake at 4:00, so I told Johnny I'd meet him back at the Cat by 6:30. That would give us enough time to meet the Stool Pigeon by 7:00. He agreed and I hit the road again.

Mariani's funeral home was packed, inside and out. The line of cars was fifteen deep before you even got to the parking lot entrance. The cops were called in to direct traffic on both ends of DePasquale Avenue. I'm sure they liked that.

After the wait in traffic and then finally finding a spot to park, I still had to stand in a line outside that went halfway around the building before I even made it to the entrance. Once inside, the wait was still another fifteen to twenty minutes to make it to the room that Carmine was waked in. Carmine would have loved to see it.

While scanning the people in the slow-moving line ahead of me, I got a kick out of the mix. Unknowingly, Judges stood next to ex-cons, while strippers stood with Sunday school teachers. It was a sight to see.

We were tipped off ahead of time that the Feds broke in the night before and wired the funeral home with surveillance cameras and audio bugs. I'm glad that Carmine's wife, Carla, knew nothing about it.

The Code

Jimmy the Weasel was up ahead and motioned for me to come up to where he was in line. Grace was already inside waiting for me so I thought about it for a second then decided to just wave politely. Fuck him.

As I creeped ahead slowly, my head turned to the left just in time to view a private room that contained Nicholas and Emma, sitting stone faced and being consoled by Carmine's sister Marie, the only one who didn't marry.

Finally, it was my turn to sign the guest book.

What the Hell should I write? From Nicholas Mancusso? The guy that slit your throat?

As I finally entered the wake room, I was faced with three easels jam-packed with photographs. Leaning in to view them up close, I could see that I was in ninety -percent of them.

Carmine's first communion, Carmine sledding on Neutaconkanut Hill, Carmine's bachelor party, Carmine's this and Carmine's that. I was in almost every one! It was like my life was up on those easels too!

My attention was diverted to the whaling sound of Carla Torro, grieving uncontrollably over the loss of her husband, the man I whacked.

All eyes were on me, as it was my turn to approach the casket.

I stood there, gazing. *An open fuckin' casket! I can't believe it! No way in Hell did I ever expect this coffin to be open! No way!*

My eyes stayed focused on the kneeling thing as I stood directly in front of the coffin. I forget what they called that thing. The stool! The kneeling stool!

I kneeled down on it, without looking up.

Everyone knew Carmine and I were best friends. The room full of seated spectators were burning a hole in the back of my neck with their more than nosey eyes.

I'll bet everyone's waiting for me to break down! What should I do? Should I force a cry? Whatever you do, keep your eyes down and don't look up at Carmine.

I folded my hands together and bowed my head.

Okay, um..., Our Father, who art in heaven, hollowed be Thy... Holy shit! Nicky, you looked up! Damn it, Nicky, you looked! I brought my folded hands up to my mouth and stared in silence. Then waited a few more seconds and made the sign of the cross.

Look at his skin? It looks fake! His suit looks nice, that's the one he wore at my and Grace's last wedding anniversary dinner, I think. His hair looks funny though. He doesn't wear it like that. What's up with that?

Is that his neck? His real neck? The one I slashed? What

did they use, body filler or something? Amazing. Carmine you stupid ass, why did you make me do this to you, why?

You would have put me in Federal prison! For life! Away from my family, for life! I should have cut off your b... and forgive us our trespasses as we forgive those who trespass against us; and lead us not into temptation, but deliver us from evil, Amen. I made the sign of the cross, again.

Carla left the receiving line— wobbly. With both hands full of crumbly and wet tissues, she met me at the casket as I was starting to stand from the kneeling thing. Everyone was watching. I embraced Carla for what seemed an eternity but she wouldn't let go of me!

She just sobbed and sobbed and sobbed, soaking my neck with tears and water-snot. I held on to her for as long as she wanted to, after all, I did this to her husband.

Peering over Carla's shoulder, I glanced at the held-up line behind us and noticed my guy Bobby Castratoro looking on and pretty much knew what he was thinking. I then scanned the room full of mourning onlookers and spotted Grace in the third row, stretching her delicate neck out above the elderly lady in front of her so I would spot her.

Carla blurted out through the cries, "Why did this

happen, Nicky, why?" I didn't answer. Instead, I side stepped the both of us to the end of the casket in front of the massive flower arrangements so the line could keep moving.

"Oh God," Carla sobbed, "will you please find out who did this monstrous thing to our beloved Carmine?" I still didn't answer.

She broke down enough for the rest of the people to leave the receiving line and huddle around her. I used that opportunity to escape the small spectacle and slip over to Grace, who was saving the seat next to her.

I kissed my wife, also in tears, and gingerly sat down in the crowded space among the rest of the mourners. Bobby C had just paid his respects to Carmine and looked over at me as he made his way to the receiving line. I wished he hadn't done that.

Grace caught me looking at my watch as people came and went throughout the evening. Bobby had left a long time before and so did the rest of my new crew. Well, the ones that came anyway.

I spotted Carla's priest coming and new it was time to leave Grace. The Catholic priests make them close the doors to the room while they say their prayers in front of the casket, trapping everyone inside to endure the longest and most boring sermon you've ever heard.

I jumped up, kissed Grace goodbye, got a look that could kill and made it out of there just in time as they were kicking the stoppers off the bottoms of the doors.

It was 6:10 and I had to get over to the club to pick up Johnny Moonlight for our meeting at 7:00, so I hustled to my pickup, dropped my keys, did the swoop, no pipe bomb, got in my truck and got away.

Traffic wasn't too bad, so I kicked back and put my favorite radio station on, quietly. Oldies-B101 was the only one I liked, except for the one that aired the ball games when the Red Sox played. The radio commercial was just ending, and they began the start of the next song. I was pretty good at guessing the songs early on with just the first few notes, and I guessed that one right away too.

It was Saturday Night Fever by the Bee Gees. Carmine and I practically lived at the discos when this song was out, when we were young and invincible.

Joined at the hip, there wasn't a moment we weren't together. Fighting in clubs, picking up girls, getting in trouble with the law and laughing about it later. We did it all. Together.

But Carmine was a rat and rats had to be exterminated. He made his own bed. He made the wrong choice and he knew the consequences. The Code of Silence, Omerta, is a sacred vow and Carmine broke that vow. And if rules aren't followed there will be utter chaos within the family, within La Cosa Nostra.

TEN

Johnny Moonlight was waiting for me in the parking lot at The Pink Pussycat when I pulled in. He hopped in my vehicle, quiet, serious.

I'd seen him like this before. He was a no-nonsense guy that took these things seriously. He didn't want to get hurt, but most importantly he didn't want me getting hurt. Johnny had been like a father to me, a mentor in a way.

When I first joined his crew, he told me to keep my head low and my nose clean. Or, vice versa, I can't remember. I do remember Johnny giving me some of his own money after I handed him my earnings one week when my Heather was born. He always looked out for me, and I knew he was worried about me that night too.

Still quiet, I broke the ice. Talking in code in case the truck was bugged, I asked Johnny a question.

"What's your guess on the winner of that race tonight?"

Translation: "Who's the stool pidgeon we gotta whack?"

"I don't know kid, my money is on that horse named Serge, from the farm on the mountain," Johnny replied.

Translation: "Not sure, maybe it's Sergio Almonte from Federal Hill."

"That's a good horse to pick, but I've seen that horse run. He's not what you think. I can't imagine him being the winner, not in a race like that. Plus, it's not his style, I'd be surprised if he wins."

Translation: "Nah."

We followed the directions correctly which got us to the location a little early.

"115 Knight Street," Johnny said, reading from the note that Billy Bath gave us.

"It is supposed to be a lumber yard or something, but it looks more like a hardware store with just that small stack of plywood and the gardening tools over there. This has to be the place. Park in front in case we need to boogie out of here quickly. Be careful, okay, kid?"

"I will. You too, Johnny."

With briefcases in hand, we approached the meeting as if we were there for just that, a meeting. My case had nothing but a stack of brochures from The Pink Pussycat in it and Johnny's was full of rope to bind the corpse in case we needed to. Oh, and one, big ass, dead, thawing rat.

The plan was for both of us to greet the target when he arrived, then one of us would shake hands with him while the other one opened fire to the back of the head, emptying all seven rounds into him before letting go of the firm grip.

Johnny found the front door key under the first porch step, just where the note said it would be. It was still a little early so we went in and cased the inside.

It was small, dimly lit and packed with small hand tools for what looked like small jobs. A rectangular table sat in the corner with three chairs tucked neatly under it. I presumed that was for us.

"Nicky, the note says for you to call Billy Bath when you get here. I'm going to take a leak outside before this guy pulls up. You make the call."

"Okay, but be careful, Johnny. Please."

"You got it."

With one eye on the parking lot, I dialed Billy's number on my cell phone. It took him a while to answer, so I figured he might be sleeping. He answered.

"Hello?"

"It's Nicky. We found the place okay but the guy hasn't arrived yet. We're ready for him though."

"Good Nicky, good. Please be careful alright?"

"No problem, Billy. We can handle it. I'll call you when it's done."

"Okay, Nicky, I'll talk to you then. Oh, I might as well tell you the target's name now that you are there."

"Go ahead, Billy, what's his name?"

"The rat that we want you to kill tonight is, Johnny Moonlight."

I looked up just as Johnny was coming through the front door zipping up his fly. The look on his face seemed to change when he saw mine. Without lowering the phone from my ear, I lowered the volume on it with my little finger.

"Billy," I said, "are you serious? Are you sure the Red Sox are thinking of trading that rookie pitcher so soon?"

"I'm sure, Nicky. Johnny is the rat. This is a direct order coming down straight from the boss. Kill Johnny Moonlight. Then send a message like we talked about. Goodbye, Nicky."

I stood there, stunned, still looking straight at Johnny. And, he was still looking back at me.

Then my phone rang again. Confused, I looked down and saw an unfamiliar number. I never answer calls like that but I was dazed, so without thinking I picked up this one, still face to face with my mentor and good friend, my target, Johnny Moonlight.

"Hello?" I said, still thinking of what I was just told.

"Nicky?" the voice sounded familiar but only vaguely.

Yeah? Who's this?" There was a pause, then an answer.

"Nicky, this is Star."

Blinking hard, I looked at Johnny and had just given away my feeling of surprise, immediately mad at myself for showing my cards.

It took me a second longer for things to sink in then my mind quickly switched from a confused state to a defensive one. The call from Billy put me into battle mode and the one from Star told me to trust no one, no one but me.

What do I do? I asked myself. *Like the good Soldier I am, I have to carry out a direct order especially from the top, no questions asked. I have to whack Johnny without hesitation! I took an oath!*

I looked down at my cell phone and then up at Johnny again, pretending to have an irritating itch that I couldn't reach on my lower back, but was really just closing the distance between my right hand and the throwaway piece that No Neck provided. The tip of my index finger touched the side of the holster.

Are there even real bullets in this gun? I wondered. *What if Johnny went outside and received the same phone call from Billy as I did and we are both to eliminate each other in a gun fight that would rival the one at the O.K. Corral?*

Johnny was still standing in the doorway, gazing at my facial expressions with a loaded nine-millimeter hand gun sitting in his back-belt gun holster.

And I stood there, frozen, while someone was on my cell phone saying she was Star, the girl that was violently murdered from a knife blade plunged deep into her eye socket. She was waiting for my reply. *What the Christ do I do!*

As I contemplated my situation, a blinding fury

began to erupt inside! I didn't like being taken for a ride, not for a minute and if I was someone's patsy, somebody would have to pay!

"Hello? How do I know this is who you say you are?" I said, raising my voice back into the phone. "I need you to prove it!"

Confused also, Johnny started nervously dancing in place while he looked anxiously out the front door and into the street, presumably waiting for someone to come pulling in any second.

"Prove it?" she said. "You want me to prove it? I need your help, Nicky! I'm in trouble, big trouble! No one knows I'm alive and I have nowhere to go. Please, please help me!"

I glanced quickly at my phone for a clue but found none.

Johnny Moonlight finally erupted! "What's going on? Who's on the phone, Kid?" Johnny was beside himself, side stepping and moving across the store-front like a nervous big cat—caged, glancing at me, then to my cell phone, then back at me and then the parking lot!

"Prove it or I'm hanging up!" I yelled, "Prove it now!"

"This is Star I'm telling you!" the nervous voice on

the phone screamed back. "You came to my rescue one night when some asshole customer refused to pay me for a lap dance! For what *you* called "His Penance," you made him give me $400.00 for a $40.00 lap dance! It's me, Nicky..., It's Star! Please help me, please!"

Then there was silence. She hung up, which made things lots worse.

"Kid, if you don't tell me right now what's going on I'm going to go postal," Johnny said, reaching around for his piece behind his back and looking back and forth between me and the parking lot behind him.

If he goes for his piece, it's all over. I'll have no choice but to drop to the floor, gun blazing with a strike force of one but equal to a shock and awe of ten. I won't stop until my gun is empty. I can still hear Billy Bath ordering me to kill Johnny Moonlight. I know I should obey that order without another thought but..., things are not right. I just can't take him out like this. I need to think!

"Johnny, please listen to me, we need to talk. Something's wrong. I think I'm being set up and used as a patsy. Maybe you are too, I don't know. Maybe you're even in on it!"

I walked slowly over to Johnny Moonlight as if to show him something on my cell phone.

"Look at this, Johnny." As he leaned forward to view my phone screen, I suddenly hauled off and cold cocked my longtime friend between the eyes with all I had, sending him reeling feebly backwards, then in a dead stop against the hard stud-wall where the rakes and garden hoses hung.

Rubbing the back of his neck and skull he sat there on the floor, reached for his gun, and pulled it from its holster behind his back where I quickly kicked it from his hand, sending it spinning and sliding across the old planked floor and under the table and one of the chairs.

A look of surprise, crossed his face. A look just before another right hook wiped it off. I then straddled my former Captain with determination and heartless vigor. Sitting on his chest, the barrel of my semi-auto fit nicely between his eyebrows just above the bridge of his bruised nose. It was strictly business.

"Now, I'm going to ask you three questions, Johnny—and I need you to swear to tell the truth to the Virgin Mary and on the souls of your little grand-children, without hesitation! If you lie, I'll know it and I swear to God I'll keep you alive long enough for you to watch and feel that fuckin' fat rat being forced into your opened mouth, inch-by-inch until just that dirty rodent's boney legs and feet are resting against your drooling, wet lips! Friend or not. I'll do it!"

"Try me, ask away," Johnny said, dazed, and glancing at the front door—closing his eyes briefly before opening them again.

"First question! Are you a fuckin' rat? Are you? Did you rat out the family too? Like Carmine?"

I asked with a sense of urgency while Johnny replied like he'd had all the time in the world.

"Never," he slowly and eventually answered, looking up at me, defiantly through blackened eyes that were starting to swell. I pushed the barrel down a little harder on his forehead.

"Second Question! Were you sent here tonight to kill me? Was I the target?"

He answered in the same, slow, and drawn-out way! "No!"

"And third! Do you know who killed that dancer they found murdered in the parking lot at the Cat that night?" I waited. I waited and watched his expression.

"I do not," he answered, deliberately and indignant. "I swear to the Virgin Mary and on my grandchildren's little souls. I do not know." He exhaled a slow but steady stream of air out of his nose. "Now, what the Christ is all this about, Nicky?"

Seemingly on the same team again, we both glanced over at the front door, not quite sure who we were expecting, if anyone at all.

Johnny rubbed his forehead where I clocked him and started to get up by planting one knee on the floor. I reached for his right hand to help him, but more importantly to tie up his trigger hand, in case I was being conned and he carried a piece in an ankle holster like I did. After that, I figured it was what it was and if he lied to me, *oh well, I lose.*

As he rose to his feet, I noticed the caller I.D. on my phone had displayed a different number than the one that Star originally gave to me. That told me nothing.

"You know, Nicky, I ought to put your fuckin' lights out for what you just did to me!" Johnny mumbled, making his way over to the table where his gun slid underneath.

"I know, I know. I just got a call from a dead girl, how do you think I feel! Let's get out of here and I'll explain later. And Johnny, if your phone rings, don't answer it, because you're dead too."

"She's dead, I'm dead, what the frig Kid, is

everybody dead around here? All except the guy we came to whack! And speaking of that guy, where is he?"

"He's not coming. There is no target. There's no meeting, no guy, no rat, no nothing. And if I'm right, there never was a rat."

ELEVEN

The sun was setting by the time Johnny Moon-light and I secured our surroundings and made it to my vehicle. Rather than drop my keys, this time I openly jumped down in a push-up position and scanned underneath it. Thoroughly.

I had Johnny search through my glove box for a band aid for the cut on his nose-bridge when suddenly my phone was laying between us on the console and rang out and surprised the living shit out of us! It was Billy, the underboss!

"Don't touch it, Johnny! You're supposed to be dead!"

"What the frig is that supposed to mean? Dead from who? By who? By you? Were you supposed to whack me, Nicky?"

Johnny sat back against his seat as my cell phone

continued ringing. "I get it now. I was the target all along, wasn't I?" I sat back in mine.

"Yeah, but I didn't know that until I got here," I answered. My phone finally stopped ringing.

"Well, that doesn't make sense, Nicky. A contract is a contract. What harm would it have done by telling you ahead of time that I was your target?"

"Exactly!" I punched the steering wheel in frustration and heard the notification of a voicemail on my phone. *Billy,* I thought.

This is the most screwed up conversation I've ever had. I'm sitting here talking with my friend who I was ordered to take out but didn't, about a girl that wanted to talk to me about my other friend who I was ordered to take out, and did.

"You'd better call him back, Nicky. Or he'll catch on."

"He's already caught on." Just then, Johnny's phone started ringing. "See? He knows I'm on to something. The problem is, I still don't know just what it is yet."

"Johnny, we are both dead men now. Listen, your car is at the club. If I take you back there for it right now, we just might get away without being noticed but within an hour they are going to have every wise guy from here to Buffalo looking for us, with the bounty saying dead or alive."

"Agreed, lets go, Nicky!"

We made it to the Cat in just under thirty minutes. The parking lot was full but remained dark because of the lamp bulb that burned out the week before. 'No Neck' was supposed to call a repairman but, as usual, he dropped the ball on that. We were glad he did.

I parked beside the dumpster in the back where Star's beamer was. I pretended to unbuckle my seat-belt, but in reality I gripped the semi-auto behind me with my right hand, just in case Johnny decided to put a bullet in my gut on the way out.

Instead, he leaned in and kissed my left cheek, thanked me for my loyalty and for believing in him when it came to the "rat" thing, and off he went.

Time went by as I sat in the dark by that dumpster. The smell from it nauseated me, but I used the offensiveness of it to hide by, unnoticed. Even with the windows rolled up tight, the stench crept in and attacked my sensitive smelling ability. I sat and I thought. It smelled, and I sat and I thought.

I must have fallen asleep because a raccoon or a cat jumped up on the dumpster and scared the shit out of me! The echo it made against its steel sides made it seem louder than it was!

Before I knew it a group of bachelor partiers left the club right at closing time, stumbling to their car, and vomiting everywhere before getting in. Just what I needed to see. Then, the last dancers left with the bouncers, along with Scammy the bartender and a few of the management who left out the side door with a few of Johnny's crew, including my own crew member, Jimmy the Weasel.

When The Pink Pussycat's neon lights finally turned off, which were apparently on a timer, the humming sound of the sign's old ballasts left the rest of the night in total silence, giving me a chance to think without distraction.

The girl on the phone was the only thing I could think of and that's just what I did. I thought of every scenario and possibility, still unable to get that putrid, rotting garbage smell out of my nostrils. And of course, I thought of my good friend Carmine, being buried in just a few hours, amongst the other Catholics in Saint Ann Cemetery in Providence.

I knew where the spare key to the club was hidden, so I turned my dome light off, quietly opened my truck door, and crept across the lot and into the entranceway where a flower planter hung on the windowsill. Under some flowers and deep inside the dark and rich soil lay the spare key. It was funny how the strippers took the time to maintain that flower box whereas the management didn't give a shit.

With cat burglar-like movements, from my youth, I entered the club and made my way to the back office where the security equipment was stored. The door was not only unlocked, but it was left wide open.

The security equipment was left unsecure too. I thought that was odd but took full advantage of it. I knew that Billy Bath had to show the Providence detectives the video from the night that Star was murdered, but the camera only caught her walking towards her Beamer and nothing beyond that because of the poor quality and the darkness beyond the camera's range. But I had to look anyway.

The search bar on the computer allowed me to enter the date and time of the murder but the light from the monitor lit up the room and left me feeling exposed and vulnerable.

I waited for the video to load, tapping the pistol in my back holster while twitching my right leg enough to remind me of the one on my ankle.

There it was, a little grainy but doable.

I got goosebumps at the back of my neck, as I watched Star walk from the back entrance to her car without a care in the world. She sure was beautiful. Her china doll haircut and exotic eye makeup was clearly visible, as she turned to wave either hello or goodbye to someone back at the door.

Who was that? I wondered, but no one came into view.

Star then turned without breaking stride which twirled the bottom of her skirt and exposing a higher portion of her legs and thighs. The stiletto shoes made her legs go on forever. Then she was gone. She faded into the darkness like a ghost, evaporating into the abyss.

I sat there, gazing at the video monitor, just imagining what was happening in that darkness. I wondered if she was suffering in endless agony or was it a quick and painless death.

Then something hit me. Figuratively speaking I mean.

I rewound the video and started it over. There was Star again walking to her car. There she was turning and waving to that unknown person and there she went continuing on to her death. I paused it. I paused it right there.

"Son of a bitch!" I said, in a slow and drawn-out whisper. "I'll be damned."

Star was beautiful alright. Beautiful from the top of her black, poker-straight hair, to her slight belly peak under her midriff shirt, then on to her sexy slit-skirt and long flawless legs showing her stiletto heels and moon shaped tattoo on her right ankle.

Whispering softer than before, I sat back in the chair. "There it is, the "moon" tattoo! This isn't Star at all, it's her twin sister, Moon! They killed Moon!"

Suddenly, lights from a car lit up the window behind the monitor! I quickly shut down the screen and ducked down just above the window sill. Luckily my pickup was on the far side of the dumpster, in the dark and out of sight. I didn't choose black as a color option for nothing.

The car doused its lights and two men got out and headed for the entrance. The darkness hid their identities so I tried to dilate my eyeballs by staring at the darkest part of the lot. It was no use though, it all happened too fast.

A car from the main road drove by the club and shined a small beam of headlights across the bottoms of the men's trousers as it went past. That's when I noticed one of the guy's shoes. Instead of tying his laces in a bow in front of his shoes, this guy tied them off to the side. Way off to the side.

I made a B-line through the office door and into the stage area where I dove behind Scammy's bar. Just in time.

The two unlocked the door, walked in and without turning on the lights, shuffled past the bar and into the office, shutting the door behind them.

I went for it. The dimly-lit room had me quietly bouncing off every stool, chair, and table as I made my way to and out the door.

With no moon out, the parking lot was even darker now, but thank God for that smelly garbage dumpster. I found my vehicle by smell rather than sight.

Of all nights, there was no way to check under my truck for a pipe bomb before getting in and that bugged me. But waiting for those two guys to find me out there bugged me more, so I inserted my key into the ignition and gently turned it until it reached the starting position and then sprung back to its resting place, all while I squinted grotesquely, biting my lower lip and waiting for the "Ka-boom!" that never came.

With headlights off, I pulled away from The Pink

Pussycat and redialed Star's phone number. She picked it up on its first ring.

"Nicky? Is that you?"

"It's me, Star. I'm so sorry about your sister, Honey. I can't imagine losing a sibling, let alone a twin."

"So, you know?"

"I know."

"Nicky, what am I going to do? That knife was meant for me! I don't know if they know that they killed the wrong girl yet, but it shouldn't take them long to. Can you help me, please?"

"Star, listen to me. Meet me at the airport tomorrow morning at 10:00 a.m. Be in the long-term parking lot across from The Dolce Luna restaurant. I'll find you. Pack enough clothes for a lifetime, Star, do you understand?"

"I understand. 10:00 a.m, I'll be there. Thank you, Nicky."

"You're welcome."

"Oh, and Nicky?"

"Yeah?"

"Do you know what Dolce Luna means in Italian?" Star asked, as she broke down, crying.

"Yes, Honey I do. It means, "Sweet Moon.""

TWELVE

Oh, no. Grace! My darling wife, Grace! I hadn't thought about her and the kids during this debacle all day!

Rushing home, my mind shot off in all directions! I had to think it through. *Start from the beginning, Nicky!*

An order comes down from the Underboss, Billy Bath. I was chosen to take out my friend, Carmine, who was deemed a rat.

Then, thinking it was Star, her twin sister Moon is whacked by mistake. Star had information for me about the murder of Carmine.

And lastly, I am chosen for another hit. The target is none other than my mentor, a highly respected Captain, Johnny Moonlight.

And, the one who gave me the contract? The

Underboss, Billy Bath, the one who gave me the first contract!

When I pulled into my driveway it had to be at least 3:00 a.m. A sadness came over me when I looked at the usual off-limits spot where my Heather and Sonny (Little Carmine) left their bikes—tipped over and sideways. They were told a million times to use the kick stands but...,

The yard seemed neat, orderly—not lived in. Something was missing and that something was me.

Even Neighborly-Neighbor was in his home, all tucked in and presumably doing the right thing. He didn't need me to straighten him out either. No one needed me.

I entered the alarm code and snuck in and upstairs. Poking my head into each of the kid's rooms I could hear Sonny breathing and smell Heathers apple-scented shampoo. *She is growing up so fast, without me.* I was riddled with guilt.

Then, I entered our bedroom and found Grace sitting up in bed, reading a romance novel by the nightlight on an end table that belonged to her grandmother Theresa. She kept her lotions and nail polish stuff on a homemade doily her grandmother made along with a picture of her and me on our honeymoon in Hawaii.

The cover of the book had a picture of an out-of-focus, dreamy guy wearing a man-bun. I hate those things.

She looked up at me with that look. The same look that she's given me each time I stayed away for too long or came home too late over the years.

"Hello, Mr. Mancusso, my long-lost husband."

"Hello, Mrs. Mancusso, my beautiful and forgiving wife." She looked over the top of her reading glasses with one eyebrow up and one down.

"Mad at me?"

"Yup," she answered, looking back down to her romance novel with the goofy man-bun guy on the cover.

"Grace, you know my job keeps me out all hours of the night sometimes! We've talked about this!"

Grace pulled off her glasses and sat up straight. "No, Nicky, you've talked about this. You told me never to question you about your job or your friends or your deals or your..., your everything! And I haven't! For years I haven't! But it's hard sometimes, Nicky!"

She put her glasses back on and attempted to start back in her book, but couldn't.

"And another thing!"

Oh boy.

"What in God's name is up with you?" Carmine was your best friend! You two were like brothers! You didn't cry like you should have! You didn't mourn or grieve like you should have! And you didn't show any interest in the murder investigation like you should have! You haven't even been there for Carla and the kids like you should have! You have a lot of making up to do, Mister! You'd better take a good look at yourself, or better yet, ask God for forgiveness tomorrow at Carmine's funeral. It starts at 10 a.m. and I think it would be nice if we all got there a little early and lit a candle for our friend."

"Funeral? The funeral is tomorrow?" *Oh God, Star!* I thought.

"You're kidding right? Nicholas Francis Mancusso, I'm so mad at you right now! Don't you dare tell me that you forgot and don't even think about being one minute late! Did you forget?"

I guess I didn't answer fast enough because 'Man-Bun' left Graces hands and came hurling at me before I had a chance to duck. The corner of the book caught me square in the nose and filled my eyes with tears immediately. It was a lucky break though, a very lucky break. That was my out.

"Oh Nicky, I'm so sorry, are you okay? I didn't mean to hurt you, darling!"

"I'm okay, Grace."

"Are you sure? I don't know what made me do that. I'm so sorry, it's just that...,"

"I know. It's okay, Honey. I deserved it. I did forget about the funeral being at 10:00 tomorrow. It's just that with my best friend's death and all, I've been running around with my head in the clouds. I even booked a charity meeting with someone tomorrow at the same time as Carmine's mass, 10:00 a.m. I'm sorry, Grace."

I wiped the water from my eyes before continuing.

"Grace, Honey, would it be okay with you if I still kept the appointment with that nice woman at 10:00 a.m., and then I'll hustle on over to the church and hopefully join you and the kids in time to receive Holy Communion? I just don't want to disappoint that woman; she could really use my help. Then she has to catch a flight, and she's not sure when she'll be back in this area again."

Grace dabbed my watery eyes with a tissue she plucked from the box on her night stand.

"Oh Nicky, of course it's okay, sweetie. I'm so sorry I hurt you."

"I'm okay now, Grace. Thanks for understanding."

After a romantic and long overdue night with my bride, I awoke at 7:30 with one thing on my mind. Star.

I took a hot shower, put on the nicely-ironed suit that Grace laid out for me and found myself thinking of Star again, when applying the new cologne I got last Christmas. Then I thought of Moon and it sickened me.

I wrote the kids a note and promised them I'd see them at the church around 10:30. Then we'd go for ice cream after the cemetery. We could take Carmine's kids too, if Carla let us.

After leaving the note on my Heather's doorknob, she being the oldest and could be counted on to read it to Sonny and show it to Mom, I went into the children's bathroom and stood on the toilet seat cover. From there, I reached up and slid over the ceiling tile overhead. Then, I felt around in the opening. I felt around until my fingers bumped a small canvass bank-bag which contained a semi-fireproof, bank deposit box. I took it down and sat on the toilet cover. After counting out ten thousand dollars in large bills and stuffing them down my pants, I buttoned things up and headed out the door.

My buddy, Neighborly-Neighbor was already up watering his lawn that didn't need watering. *What is it with this guy?* Every blade of jade-colored grass leaned toward the sun in exactly the same way, with hardly any of them out of place.

After I did my key swoop and undercarriage inspection on my truck, I looked back just in time to see my neighbor placing the garden hose on the ground and lifting a wooden handle from the ground and by his feet.

At the end of that wooden handle was a brandy-new, high-end, chrome-wheeled and silver-bladed manual push..., lawn mower!

Yup, an old fashioned, push lawn mower that doesn't make a peep! Not on T's, not on S's, not ever!

Neighborly-Neighbor looked over at me with a sense of a do-gooder pride, so I just had to give him a thumbs up! I waited for him to goofily give me one back and hopped into my truck and raced for the airport.

I arrived at the ticket counter and made sure I

wasn't followed before I did my thing. Then continued to the long-term parking lot, which was pretty
full, but I managed to find two open spaces directly
across from The Dolce Luna, which made me think
of Moon again. Sweet Moon.

Still a little early, I kicked back, put the radio
on and closed one eye. It was a good thing I didn't
close two because when my cell phone rang, I almost
hit my head on the headliner after jumping a mile!
"Ring!!!"

Looking down at it while it danced sideways across
my center console, I saw the caller's name come up
on the phone screen. It was Billy Bath!

Then, a loud knock full of knuckles rapped hard
on my side glass window, sending me into a fighting
mode and making me reach around with lightning
speed for the throwaway nine.

It was Star, looking through my window like a
scared puppy in a puppy mill, begging with pathetic
eyes like one of those late-night money raisers that
knew just when to insert the sad music in order to
pull at your heart strings.

But Star wasn't conning me. She looked like Hell.
Her mascara looked like it ran, dried, and then ran

again. A Red Sox baseball cap hid her china doll bob-cut and made her look more like a soccer mom.

No belly shirt, no short slit-skirt, and no six-inch stilettos. Just ripped jeans, sneakers, and a stretched-out Keith Urban T-shirt. *Is this the real Star that's usually under all that paint and paper?*

I motioned for her to come around and get in, which she did without hesitation. She began talking even before her butt hit the seat.

"Thank you for coming, Nicky! I didn't know what else to do, I'm so scared! My sister!" She broke down in tears so I handed her some Dunkin' napkins I had under my seat.

"Don't worry, I'll fix this. Tell me what you know about Carmine."

"Carmine? I know a lot about Carmine. I know you killed him for nothing!" My heart sank. Knowing it and hearing it was two different things.

"I killed him? What makes you think I killed him?"

"Because giving a guy a private lap dance is like being a hairdresser with a client in her chair. In the standard time of just two songs, you hear more gossip than a shop full of old biddies in a downtown set, wash and color salon.

"A few weeks back, this customer I had in the VIP room who wanted the premium dance package—a fully nude lap dance for three songs, was flashing a wad of ones around and telling me all the people he knew and just how important he was. He said if I ever needed anything he was my guy. You know the type, a wanna-be somebody."

I nodded "yes" with a disapproving look of "no." She turned and glanced out the back window before continuing.

"Anyway, this guy said he was a friend of some cousin of Nunzio's."

"No Neck, that fat bastard," I added.

"Yes, well, he said that he knew all the guys, you know, the "guys" and started rattling them off. I just let him show off and worked him for more money. I just figured he liked to hear himself talk until..."

"Until what?"

"Until he blurted something out about Carmine." She hesitated and checked out things through the rear window again.

"Like what, Star. What about Carmine."

"Nicky, I'm scared! Scared of what happened to my sister will happen to me!"

"I won't let that happen, Star. Trust me. Tell me what he said!"

"Okay, he said there was a Captain of a crew that was being set up as a rat, he didn't say why. He just said that the patsy they were going to use to whack him was the guy that would replace him as Capo and that they were great friends. I asked him how he knew that and he just said that Nunzio has "diarrhea of the mouth." Plus, he knows these things."

"What else."

"I just thought the guy was a blowhard and didn't think much about it until, well you know, Carmine was killed and then I saw all those guys congratulating you that day while I was dancing on stage with my sister, Moon." Her voice became real soft and shaky.

"One last question, Honey. You were supposed to meet me in your Beamer that night. How did Moon end up in your car instead of you? And how did they mistake you for her?"

"My sister grabbed a cab and stopped in the club sometime before closing that night. She sometimes did that. We were able to come and go without being distinguished because most people couldn't tell us apart.

"That night, whoever was at the front door didn't know if it was her or me going in and out and probably didn't care. My sister came downstairs as I was cleaning up to go home. She wanted to take me to an after-hours club for our birthday. Always sweet like that. She volunteered to drive and said that was part of my birthday present. The other part was a card she handed me that I put in my locker for safe keeping but left without. I left the birthday card from my sister there, Nicky!"

She sobbed uncontrollably as a stream of tears flowed down her cheeks, off her chin, and onto her Keith Urban T-shirt which pooled up onto her endless cleavage before disappearing into the unknown. Her hands trembled pitifully like that puppy in the puppy mill—and before I knew it, her face was resting comfortably against my chest, nestled in with eyes closed and both her hands in one of mine.

This is where I always get in trouble, I thought to myself. *It never fails!*

THIRTEEN

After Star got her things and locked up her car, she sat back in mine and waited for my instructions. "I bought you a one-way ticket to Denver. It's a four-and-a-half-hour flight with a layover in Minnesota. Once you get there, you'll call this number and ask for a guy named Tony. He knows you're coming and will pick you up when you land. He's a good guy and you can trust him."

"Where will I stay, Nicky?"

"Don't worry, Tony owes me a favor and this is it. He'll put you up until you get your own apartment— he also knows you're a dancer, so he can get you a gig right away if that's what you want to do. Here's ten grand to get you on your feet."

I handed her the envelope and she just stared at it, motionless,–jaw opened.

"I...I don't know what to say? How can I ever repay you, Nicky?"

"Just stay safe and maybe find some rich guy to latch onto. The ticket's in the envelope too. Send me a post card when you get settled and let me know how you're doing, but make sure it's postmarked from another city. You'd better get going now."

"Thank you, Nicky. I will never forget you." She leaned over, kissed my cheek and then she was gone.

My phone rang from a blocked caller. I wasn't sure if I should pick it up or not—thinking it was Billy or one of his cronies like No Neck or Stephano Montella from Johnny's crew, but I said "frig it" and answered it anyway. Stephano Montella was from Italy and highly respected as a no-nonsense guy, like Johnny Moonlight. Montella's nickname was "the zip." Any Italian Mafioso living here in America were called zips by our guys.

"Hello?" I said, loud and forcefully. I figured I'd better sound unintimidated just in case.

"Skipper, it's Friday Night. Where the Hell are you? You've got half of Rhode Island looking for you! I don't know what you did, but Billy Bath says you've got to come in. He wants the crew to find you and bring you in. Johnny Moonlight is AWOL as well and they have an APB on him too! What the fuck, Skipper?"

"Calm down, Friday. It'll be fine. Where are you and who's with you?"

"We are at the diner, Skipper. Your whole crew is here! Iron Mike, Bobby C and the Saccoccia Brothers, all except Jimmy the Weasel. He's been MIA ever since that girl was killed."

"Yeah, he might be with them, I don't know."

What do we do Skipper, you know we can't go against the boss. What did you do, man?"

"Find a quiet corner and put me on speaker phone. I've got something to say to you guys."

"Okay, give us a second."

As I waited, I started my pickup and headed for the highway. Looking up to the sky, I noticed a plane climbing on takeoff and wondered if Star was on board and on her way to a brand-new life.

Friday spoke. "Okay we're back, Skipper, you're on speaker phone."

"Alright. I'm not going to tell you guys what to do. You're on your own. And I'm not telling you to put yourself in jeopardy by disobeying an order from the top either. You all know what will happen if you get caught helping me.

"What I am saying is if any of you choose to come after me, I won't hold it against you. You just need to know that I won't go down without a fight. I was used as a patsy to whack your former Capo Regime, Carmine Torro. He was accused under false pretenses of being a stoolie and in turn ruining his honor and getting himself killed. Also, an innocent girl got knifed to death because she knew too much. And lastly, my former Captain, Johnny Moonlight— standup guy, was also put on a hit list and falsely accused of being a rat, dishonoring him and his family as well.

"The codes we live by are all we have guys. Without them we are nothing. Our codes are many—and loyalty and honor are among them.

"So do what you must, but know that I'll be waiting. 'Buona fortuna.' (Good luck.)" I hung up without waiting for a reply.

I had a plan but not a good one. If I could get to the boss and fill him in on his Underboss's doings, I just might convince him to take a look at this bogus informant that is feeding Billy that bullshit and exonerate Johnny of the false allegations. Santini is the only one that could pardon Johnny Moonlight. And me, Nicky Mancusso for that matter!

I took the Charles Street exit and raced for the

church. Carmine's funeral was forty-five minutes under way and I prayed to God that it started late. The church had to be packed because there wasn't an empty spot in sight—so I double parked aside a limo and threw the guy a C-Note.

I was right, the church was packed. Grace was nowhere in sight but I just knew she was somewhere in that seated mob, watching the entrance with glaring eyes hot enough to melt the marble statue of Saint Rocco on the pedestal beside me.

Finally, I spotted my Heather at the end of a pew, looking so grown up in her little plaid dress with dress shoes to match. Sonny sat just inches away from his sister because of the overcrowding, and I just knew that it bugged him.

Then, just as I predicted, with head turned exorcist-like towards me and with piercing eyes trained on mine, sat my beautiful wife Grace, waiting patiently for her wonderful husband.

I'm fuckin' dead, I thought. *I know that look!*

I made my way through the endless globs of patrons, some young, some old, but all there to pay their respects to Carmine and his family. I finally reached mine.

The kids both kissed me as I slid into the

tightly-packed pew. Grace didn't. She just pulled the kneeler down on cue and did the sign of the cross with the rest of the people about to pray. I had to catch up. There's nothing worse than falling behind on the sign of the cross and having to rush it to catch up. Mrs. Delfino, the seamstress from Bond Street watched me do it and looked on with disapproval.

I must have missed all the nice things they said about Carmine because the priest was already at the Holy Communion part of the ceremony. That told me I was really late.

As Father Mario approached the casket and faced the assembly with chalice in hand, people rose to form two lines and began waiting for their turn to receive the body of Christ, Holy Communion.

Grace rose with the children to exit the pew and stepped in line. I thought I might get away with skipping that part but was easily persuaded with just one look from her. As I rose, I caught some kid behind me staring at my back where I still had No Neck's 9 millimeter under my shirt, so I pulled the shirt down further and shot back a stare to the kid that said "Fuck off!"

My turn eventually came. As I approached the alter, Father Mario looked me in the eye as he reached into the chalice, pulled out a wafer, and held it up to the Heavens before offering me the offering.

Does he know? He looks like he knows. It feels like the whole church behind me knows!

The priest lowered the Host and held it out in front of my face.

"The Body of Christ," he said, awaiting my response.

"Amen," I replied, opening my mouth and allowing him to place it on my tongue. Some people have it placed in the palm of their hand for fear of spreading germs but I'm old-school and still do it the old-fashioned way.

I finished up by making the sign of the cross and turned to follow the line back to my pew. That's when I passed Carmine's casket. It was draped in a cotton white sheet with a large, red cross on it.

As I passed, I imagined Carmine throwing the coffin cover open and sitting straight up for all to see and hear! Then I pictured him pointing at me as I walked past him, screaming to the onlookers in a deep and God-like voice that echoed immensely through the hallowed church and all the way up to the rafters!

"He did it!" Carmine yelled, with two fingers

pointing to me while sitting up in the casket. "He murdered me! My best friend murdered me and it was for something I didn't do!"

Shaking my head of the horrible thought, I continued to walk past and on to my seat where I kneeled, said the 'Our Father' prayer and made the sign of the cross again before sitting back in my pew and gazing at Carmine's closed casket.

Just beyond the casket sat Nicholas, Carmine's son—my namesake and godson. Our eyes met while the look in his were one of a lost soul. Carmine was Nicholas's hero and protector, and my role as his godfather meant that I had to step in and assume that roll now. I was ready to do whatever I needed to do to help Nicholas overcome the tragic loss of his dad. Nicholas continued to look right through me.

The mass ended with my wife and countless others in tears. Grace held my hand as we followed the casket out of the church, a sign that I was forgiven.

The funeral procession looked like it was a half-mile long, so I snuck ahead of another vehicle in order to beat Grace and the kids to the cemetery. I wanted to be able to show Grace that I could get there on time and do something right.

The procession rolled down Westminster Street

and up Washington. I was about the fifth car in line behind the family's limo.

As I passed the Convention Center, I noticed a dark gray unmarked police car waiting to pull out after I passed. But he didn't wait. He lit up his hidden lights and pulled out into the procession right behind me! Then, kept his lights on as he rode my bumper presumably trying to get me to pull over!

After a few seconds of that harassment, I decided to leave the line and turn onto Chestnut Street with the unmarked vehicle following me up close until I stopped in an empty parking lot.

What now? I thought, as I lowered my window and reached for my license and registration from my glove compartment. Because of my constant harassment by the police, I kept them right on top along with my insurance papers. I sensed the cop getting out of his vehicle and walking to my truck.

I found my paperwork right away, so I sat back in my seat and straightened them as I waited for his arrival to my window. He must have already been standing just out of my view because, "Whack!" I never saw it coming!

It must have been a billy club but it felt like a sledge hammer! And that's all I remember.

FOURTEEN

The light that came through the slits in my eyes blinded me from the world, throwing my heart rate into a high rev that immediately started me on damage control and scheming for a way out.

My ears didn't seem to work—as I couldn't feel or hear anything from them at all. I did have use of my tongue though, that much I knew. It collected blood from the inside of my mouth as it darted in and out of the empty tooth socket, searching for the missing one that was there that morning.

Where am I? I thought, wondering if the semi-auto was still in my belt.

A loud ringing sound appeared in my right ear, proving that I salvaged some hearing, but the pounding in my head distracted me from all else and tried to make little things like hearing seem minuscule. And my body? It hurt. It hurt everywhere.

Why can't I turn my neck?

The breathing that I couldn't control aggravated my ribs, and I knew they just had to be broken. Holding my breath didn't help either, it just made me cough and spit up blood through my mouth and nose. So, I tried to think more instead.

Wiggle your fingers and toes, I told myself–and did with some success but they were vibrating, vibrating as if their circulation was completely cut off.

And that screaming! Oh, Madonna! What is that? Someone or something was screaming like a rabbit at the butcher shop, watching and waiting for its turn under the meat clever! It was like a bad dream I couldn't wake up from! *What is that fuckin' squeal!*

"Well, well, well," a pompous voice sounded over those God-awful screams—out of view from somewhere behind me or off to the side, I couldn't be sure. "Well, if he isn't awake, finally! You're just in time for the second half of the show! Wake up, Nicky Boy! Better get your wits about you or you'll miss it!"

My hearing was getting better but my eyesight was still blurred. Blinking fast to wipe away the sticky blood and wet tears didn't help, so I blinked long and hard— trying to push the fluids back down into the bottom of my eye sockets and away from my pupils. Still, the screams continued, hitting high notes I didn't think existed and raising the hairs on my exposed shoulders and cold neck.

Block it out, block it all out, I said to myself. *Take inventory and assess the situation.* Suddenly the screams turned to sobs. Then to soft whimpers—until eventually there was silence. Dead silence. About ten quieter minutes went by —then I must have passed out again, for how long, I don't know.

"Hey, Nicky Boy! Looky, looky! Looky see what I got!" I could hear him but I couldn't see him. The voice sounded familiar but the throbbing head pain kept me from concentrating on more than a few things at a time, so I focused on the piece in my back belt-holster under my shirt.

Tilting my head forward was painful but I managed to drop it just enough to see my situation, which I then knew wasn't good. First of all, I was sitting on a metal folding chair, shirtless, so forget about my gun. It was gone. Blood spatter stained my skin from my face to my waistline, which indicated unknown injuries.

Second, my hands and feet were tied with wire ties

that were so tight it was the reason for the pins and needles feeling in my extremities.

And third, the reason I couldn't move my neck was because it was in a metal collar, the kind of collar you'd see in those weirdo dominatrix flics. There was a chain on it that hooked to a clasp on my end, while the other end was bolted to a red-stained cement floor about ten-feet away and behind me.

Without moving my head, I shifted my eyes from left to right. The room looked like a cross between a meat locker and a playroom for S and M games. There were scores of sex toys that were used for pain that hung from the four walls to the ceiling. Some of them I couldn't even guess what they were used for!

Spikes, lots of pointy spikes. Belts, whips, and chains. Pain devices that I didn't understand. Horse mouth-bits and even stirrups with sharp, star shaped spurs!

What a bunch of sick fucks we have here, I thought. *I can't wait to meet the ring master of this freak show.*

"What do you think, Nicky Boy? Don't you want to see what I got?"

I can't friggin' wait, I thought, while my tongue poked in and out of my missing tooth socket again, hoping that maybe it was just my tooth he was dying to show me.

The unknown whack job finally walked in with an excited skip in his step as he came into view and presented himself to me. Then he slid a closed-lid box over to me which stopped a foot or so away on the red-stained concrete floor.

I didn't know which surprised me more, the fact that the familiar voice belonged to none other than Lieutenant Detective Howie Bergle of the Providence Police Department or the fact that upon looking down at his shoes, I noticed the same "off to the side" shoe laces that I spotted one of the guys wearing when I broke into The Pink Pussycat that night.

"What's up with the shoe laces, Bergle? Mommy didn't teach you how to tie your shoes? When I first met you, I knew you were an asshole, but I didn't have you pegged for a freak! Let me guess, the other guy that I saw you with at the club last night was Billy Bath? Is he your partner? Are the two of you in on some kind of conspiracy together or something? Is Billy a closet freak like you too?"

The lieutenant replied, "You're getting warmer! Tell me, Nicky Boy, how did you figure that things weren't on the level?"

"Well, Johnny Moonlight told me that the police informant told Billy Bath that Carmine's wife chose Arizona to relocate to in a witness protection program. I know that Carla would never choose such a dry and arid place to live in. Carla has asthma. There is no witness program. There is no informant. You made the whole thing up but, unfortunately, I figured it out too late. Carmine was never a rat. The only thing that I haven't figured out yet is why? Why all the bullshit? How did setting up Carmine help you in anyway?"

"Open the box, Nicky Boy, and I'll tell you. Oh wait, you can't. You're all tied up! Hold on, I'll help you!"

Bergle bent down and opened the flaps on the cardboard box. Then looked up at me with a sick smile before lowering his hands into it to remove the contents inside.

"Do you want to guess whose head I'll be pulling out? You know it must be a head. You've seen enough movies to know that there's always a head in the box! Right?" He broke out in laughter as he reached in deeper. "Whoohoo! Go ahead, take a guess! Who's screams did you wake up to as they were losing their...

nah, never mind, that's too cliché." He paused before lifting it up. Then continued.

"Is it...!" he paused again— speaking in a slow childish mimic before continuing.

"Is it..., Star's head? Did I get to her before she boarded that plane, Nicky Boy? Did you think the police didn't know about that? Such a beautiful head on that girl!"

I remembered the .380 I had strapped to my ankle. My legs were numb but I was hopeful he didn't find it and it would still be there. After flexing my leg calf to detect the ankle-holster I still wasn't sure.

"I do give you credit for figuring out that it was Moon that got the shank that night instead of Star though. Come on now! You're not playing the guessing game correctly!" He lifted it up from the box a little higher.

"Is it..., Carla? Did I get to her after the burial in her time of sorrow? And lop *her* lovely head off? Go on, guess!"

While he played his little game, I focused on my ankle and wondered. *Can I reach the gun with my hands tied together like this? I have to try!*

Finally, he lifted the contents halfway out where

just a blood-soaked neck was exposed, dripping red droplets from it and into the box.

"Oops! It's upside down! That's not fair! You'll never guess it that way! Okay hold on! Let me spin it around. Tell me the truth now! Were you going to guess your lovely wife? Come on! Tell! Is it..., Grace!!"

I squirmed frantically in my seat, estimating the length of the chain that was attached to my neck and over to the floor behind me. I figured the chain was five feet long and almost at its limit whereas the distance Lieutenant Screwball was to me was more like eight! *I'd never make it to him. I'd be like a running dog, stopped on a dime by a short chain and a tight choker!*

"Ready or not, Nicky Boy! Here it comes!"

As he lifted the head completely out of the box I sat there stunned. Stunned and lost for the words. Frothy blood dripped from it, profusely, and the game was over. It was surely over.

The box..., the box contained the head of... no other than..., Billy Bath, the underboss of the family! *Holy shit.* My heart skipped a beat but again, yet, I showed no emotion.

In an act of defiance, I stared at Billy's head as that whack job spun it like a basketball, and still I stared. He squeezed Billy's cheeks and used him as a ventriloquist's dummy, and still I stared. He pretended that Billy spoke to me in a high pitched, Pee Wee Herman-type voice.

"Hi Nicky, how's it hanging? Huh Ha! Hut hut!" Still, I just stared.

Just then, and out of nowhere, skipped into the room, the real accomplice to all the sick shit of that sick bastard. It was the mastermind, the architect, the head monster! Standing before me, with spots of red blood on his neatly polished wing tipped shoes was the cause of all that screaming. It was my trusted and loyal mentor! It was Johnny, Johnny Moonlight!

"What do you think, kid? Confused?" Johnny asked, as I looked straight ahead, refusing to show respect by looking him in the eye.

"Not really," I answered, in a nonchalant, who gives a shit, tone. "You had me buffaloed at one point but it all makes sense to me now."

"Johnny, let's get on with the game," Bergle said, tossing Billy's head back and forth between his hands before placing it back into the box.

"Shut up you idiot!" said Moonlight. "I told you before to lay off the cocaine! Put the lid back on that damn thing and don't interrupt! Go on, kid, go on!" I focused on the wire ties cutting into my skin on my wrists, still thinking about the piece I hoped I still had in my ankle-holster. I played along with Johnny to gain more time.

"Okay, I'll tell you what I think, Johnny. In your twisted mind, you'd get what you want by getting the Underboss out of the way so you can move up the ladder and ultimately move into the boss's seat."

"You knew that any standup guys would never allow that, so we had to be eliminated. Me, Carmine, and eventually Billy Bath."

You had Officer Numb Nuts here tell Boss Santini and Billy Bath that Carmine was an informant for the FBI.

"*You're doing good, Kid. Go on!*"

"And Johnny, you knew I wouldn't whack you if I had my doubts. Then all you had to do was wait until I was tracked down by my own crew for disobeying orders. Am I close?"

"Nicky! You're right on!" Johnny said, with a smirk and a nod, while Bergle played a drum tap on top of the box containing Billy's head.

I continued. "And Lieutenant Weirdo's payoff is simple. When his partner, meaning you, Johnny Moonlight becomes the boss, he gets free rein over the narcotics distribution in New England and any other creepy market that might tickle his fancy, all the while with complete police protection."

"Then, all you had to do is get us to kill each other off so you wouldn't have to. How am I doing so far?"

"Not bad, Nicky boy! It's a shame you couldn't be around to reap the 'bennies,' kid! It's too bad. You could have been less of a threat by being less honorable. Don't you know that standup guys finish last? Fuck that code shit! It's all bullshit! I make the fuckin' rules now! Me! Johnny Moonlight! Soon to be head of the family!"

Bergle switched on a radio. The volume was already way up loud and pounded out a Led Zeppelin song, Whole Lotta Love. It was at the chaotic part of the song and went right along with the chaos that filled the room.

Johnny pounded his chest like a silverback ape, then picked a bone saw from a metal table while Bergle pulled out a fillet knife from a sheath and tested the blade for sharpness by flicking his thumb over the edge—then both, smiling from ear to ear, each took steps closer to me— knife and saw in hand.

I was determined not to scream like Billy Bath did. So, I tightened my abs, figuring they were going to slice me on my upper, shirtless torso first. Then, disembowel me alive.

But I was wrong, sicko Bergle ran the bone saw across my knee, tearing my pant leg and some skin. He set the saw on my leg again, giggling like a child, with Whole Lotta Love ending strong, filling the room with silence. I realized then that it wasn't a radio but a tape, a torture tape. *Sick Fucks.*

Bergle continued to giggle as Johnny Moonlight became inpatient. "Come on, Lieutenant! Start sawing!" Bergle pulled back on the saw!

I thought of the .380 strapped to my ankle that I couldn't reach. I thought about Grace and little Sonny and my Heather! My Heather.

After taking a deep breath, I spoke, calmly and coolly.

"Sounds like you clowns got it all figured out, except you're forgetting one thing."

"And what would that be?" Johnny asked with a grin from ear to ear, flicking the knife blade against his thumb, checking the sharpness again.

"There will always be standup guys willing to pledge their lives for La Cosa Nostra," I said. "And no matter what, will follow the rules that have to be followed. And you Johnny Moonlight didn't follow the rules. Oh, and by the way, standup guys do finish first. When they follow the code. Right Jimmy? Right, Jimmy the Weasel?"

"What the fuck are you talking about?" Johnny replied "What about Jimmy the Weasel?"

"Look behind you, ass-wipe."

Moonlight and Bergle then slowly turned around, shocked to see the Weasel, No Neck Nunzio and my entire crew standing behind them with guns drawn in a fighting stance.

"What the fuck is this?" Moonlight complained, looking to Lieutenant Bergle for backup!

Jimmy the Weasel spoke, keeping a double-barreled, sawed-off shotgun trained on their faces while No Neck disarmed their visibly stunned asses, then gave directives they didn't like.

"Don't move a muscle, ladies, or your mama won't even recognize you when asked to identify your butt-ugly bodies."

"How dare you!" Moonlight hollered. "You got a lot of nerve drawing down on a Made Guy! I'm a Captain! That's considered a death wish!"

Suddenly, all eyes trained on one man.

From the small army of eight, stepped forward a 5'1" unassuming little man with a partially squashed

—macaroni or blood-stained fedora, overstretched suspenders, and a wrinkled and yellowed, white shirt! The outdated, gray cuffed pants and meticulously polished, 1940's style winged-tipped shoes gave him away!

Without uttering a word, Antonio Carlo Santini removed the unlit Stogie from the inside of his stubbly cheek, as he took concerned inventory of the pain inflicting implements hanging on the walls around him. When he was done, he spoke.

"Johnny Moonlight," Santini said, "My most loyal Capo. Did I fail you somehow?"

"Not at all Mr. Santini, this is all a big mistake! Let's talk it over in your office tomorrow over a nice cup of espresso!"

Johnny held both his hands out in a gesture of good faith as he smiled forcefully at the little man.

"Nicky Mancusso is the traitor, Mr. Santini! An enemy of the family of whom I've been so devoted and loyal to all of my life! I'll explain this mistake and everything else to you, trust me!"

With his old wooden cane, Antonio Santini plucked a spiked, leather collar from a wall-hook— inspected it for a brief moment by testing the sharp points, then placed it back on the hook again from which it came.

"A mistake," Santini replied. "I've always believed that everyone is entitled to make a mistake."

The boss of a family would never be seen or involve himself in a situation like that. Showing up like he did is unheard of.

The boss quietly spoke again.

"Mikey and Bobby, take Johnny Moonlight out to the Roger Williams Zoo after midnight. Tell the night keeper I sent you. Feed Johnny Moonlight to the lions. Make sure he's alive when you do it."

He then stuck the unlit cigar back inside his cheek before continuing on.

"As for this fancy cop?" Do what you want with him. You may use these bizarre toys if you wish, he may like it but make sure he suffers in the end. Bury him in my garden where I plant my tomato plants. Then, bring me his cogliones," (*Testicles*).

Jimmy and Friday Night cut my zip ties while Iron Mike and Bobby removed the steel collar from my neck. And, of course, the dumb-ass Saccoccia brothers checked out the sex toys on the walls before taking the two condemned men away, as they pleaded pitifully for mercy.

"Nicky, you and I will talk tomorrow, and you will drink espresso," Santini said, as he walked with Nunzio to the door.

"Yes, Mr. Santini,." I replied, rubbing my chafed wrists and checking to see that my .380 was in fact still hidden beneath my Levi's pant leg. Safe and sound.

I went home to Grace and she tended to my wounds that night. But not before I stopped by the club to get that birthday card that Star left in her locker. The one she received from her sister Moon, the night she was slaughtered with a dagger to the eye. I mailed it to my friend Tony in Denver with the instructions that Star was to get it.

The next morning, I went to see the boss.

Like a good Soldier, I sat and listened to Santini's teachings and wisdoms. His knowledge of life was surprising to me. He explained that he had Jimmy the Weasel tail me after the funeral, knowing that Johnny Moonlight would show up one way or another.

Through the smoke which hung lazily in the air, I noticed a new shelf under the picture of Frank Sinatra.

Upon that shelf sat a decorative saucer. It was

bone-white in color with robin-egg blue, Chinese writings on it.

In that ornate saucer, proudly sat and displayed a pair of dank and moist, human remains.

"Nicola," Santini asked. That's what he called me when he was happy. "I see you admire La Coglioni."

"La Coglioni?" I asked.

"Yes, Cogliones," Santini said. "Balls!"

I learned to like espresso like he expected me to.

FIFTEEN

SEVEN YEARS LATER

I woke up early one morning just as the sun peered through the Venetian blinds and made lighted slots on the bedroom carpet. They reminded me of the slots on the utility closet door in the kitchen. After all these years I still woke up thinking of Carmine and that eventful summer all those years ago.

I was meeting No Neck—yes, No Neck for a game of golf. We'd become good friends and I must say his hygiene has greatly improved, since I've taken him under my wing and advised him on the art of romance. Old fashioned style.

After quietly creaking down the stair steps and shuffling into the kitchen for Grace's famous, ground coffee, I decided to finish writing my annual letter, my seventh one, to Star while it was quiet and Grace was still asleep.

As usual it was short and to the point. After a big gulp of coffee and with my eyes shifting back and forth from the staircase to the letter, I began to read quietly out loud.

> Dear Star,
>
> "I can't believe that Seven years have passed. Things are good with me and Grace. She still gets mad at me at times but seems to get over it quickly, especially since I don't forget to compliment her on things anymore. I never took over Billy Bath's job as Underboss after his disappearance nor did I want to. I like staying right where I am, the Captain of a small motley crew of standup guys. The kids are young adults now. My Heather is going to college in the fall and Sonny (Little Carmine) is talking to a recruiter from the Marine Corps. Now, there's an organization with codes! Carmine's widow, Carla, still sells houses, and Emma is in

high school. And, Nicholas? Remember Carmine's boy? He wants to be a doctor. His ambition is to shoot for a med-school right here in Providence. Brown University! His father would surely have been proud. To learn the ropes, I called in a favor and had Nicholas working as sort of an intern at Doctor Buonanno's office last summer. This summer will be Grace and my twentieth wedding anniversary, and I would love for you to come out with your daughter Nicki. I'll send you an invitation. Hope all is well.

All the best,
Nicky

I sat back in my chair, sipped on more of Grace's brew and reminisced about my life. I thought I barely heard "old Neighborly-Neighbor," quietly trimming the edges of his lawn with his hand-held grass scissors. *I can't forget to bring him home a Nutty Buddy after church tomorrow.*

Some of the more important people in my life are gone now but all in all, I'm happy. I do miss Carmine though. I miss the old times.

Still, after all these years, I can't come into my kitchen without glancing over at the utility closet and imagining dead Carmine jumping out to scare the living shit out of me with his long nails and boney fingers. It's probably a habit I'll never break out of.

I finished the last drop of coffee from my "World's Greatest Dad" cup, set it in the sink and made a parting glance at the closet as I passed by the shuttered door.

I thought I heard Grace get up. There was a flushing sound from the bathroom toilet upstairs so I paused to listen, when, *"Crack!!!"*

The utility closet's door swung open before me and slammed hard against the doorjamb! A dark figure in a dark face mask lunged from the closet and shot me in my neck with a stun gun that brought me to the floor in a merciless slam!

The massive amount of volts paralyzed my entire body, leaving me laying helplessly and feebly on my back and unable to move a muscle no matter how much I tried!

Puddles of drool filled the corners of my mouth while sporadic nerve twitches erupted everywhere!

Then the dark figure sat hard on my chest, pulled

a scalpel from its back pocket, and removed its facemask.

"Look at me! Look at me!" the culprit demanded— then disturbingly stared into my eyes, took the glistening blade, and slowly cut my throat from one end of my neck to the other until a two-inch gash opened up, oozing clots of blood and fluids from my inner self.

"Do you know why I'm doing this to you? Do you?" I still could not move.

Then, using forefinger and thumb, both sides of my cheeks were squeezed tightly together until my lips parted and my mouth opened wide.

"You are a murderer and this is what happens to murderers! Open your mouth! Open It!"

From his shirt pocket, a photograph of Carmine was pulled and put before my eyes for me to see. I still couldn't move. It was then placed over my lips and the center of the picture was pushed straight back into my drool-filled mouth and all the way to the back of my throat! Two fingers kept pressure on it while my eyes opened wider!

"Do you know why?" The unmasked killer waited impatiently for my reply. "Do you?!"

I nodded my head but could only mouth the

words as I looked back into his cold and empty eyes before slowly slipping away.

I barely whispered. "Yes. I know why, Nicholas, my godson." Again, only mouthing the words, as my world began to fade.

"I know why."

$$+ + + + +$$

Book 2

MAKING BONES

Coming Soon

 Bobby DePalo is a retired entrepreneur who built and led his company for 37 years before selling it and stepping back in 2023. In 1999, a life-altering accident left him paralyzed—an experience that initially set him back but ultimately fueled his determination. Against the odds, Bobby rebuilt momentum and scaled his business to a point of lasting pride.

He is the author of several books, including *A Promise*, *More Promises*, *The Code*, and his forthcoming work, *Making Bones*. His most popular and deeply personal title, *Kantfly: A Paraplegic's Story*, is a self-help memoir that offers an unfiltered look into his private journey and resilience.

www.ingramcontent.com/pod-product-compliance
Lightning Source LLC
Chambersburg PA
CBHW061324200626

46813CB00017B/2957